W9-CFQ-360

E 6

WITHDRAWN

5/09

WHERE IT LIES

WHERE IT LIES

K. J. Egan

MINOTAUR BOOKS ★ NEW YORK

This is a work of fiction. All of the characters, organizations, and events portrayed in this novel are either products of the author's imagination or are used fictitiously.

A THOMAS DUNNE BOOK FOR MINOTAUR BOOKS.
An imprint of St. Martin's Publishing Group.

www.thomasdunnebooks.com
www.stmartins.com

Book design by Rich Arnold

Library of Congress Cataloging-in-Publication Data

Egan, K. J.
    Where it lies / K. J. Egan.—1st ed.
       p. cm.
   ISBN-13: 978-0-312-53888-0
   ISBN-10: 0-312-53888-X
  1. Country clubs—Fiction. 2. Golf courses—Employees—Fiction.
3. Murder—Investigation—Fiction. I. Title.
   PS3554.A4448W47 2009
   813'.54—dc22

                           2009004502

First Edition: May 2009

10 9 8 7 6 5 4 3 2 1

*To Barbara and Ben for sticking with me, and to
the Saturday night gang for being who they are*

WHERE IT LIES

ONE

THE FIRST THING I remember about that morning was
the dog. It was a mutt, a mangy mutt, and though my friend
Danica would correct me and explain that *mangy* refers to
mange, a skin disorder that did not afflict this particular dog,
I stick by my description. It mixes alliteration and poetic li-
cense like a, well, like a mangy mutt.

Nothing else seemed amiss as I rolled into the caddie
yard, and even a dog nosing at the door to the cart barn
didn't qualify as something amiss. I knew the dog. His name
was Duke, and he belonged to Rick Gilbert, the club's head
greenskeeper, who lived in a cottage surrounded by a thick
wall of arborvitae at the far end of the parking lot. Duke
was nasty in the way that small dogs often are. In the after-
noons, he would burst through the arborvitae and snarl at
any golfer whose ball landed too close to his territory. But
in the mornings, Duke was mellow, curled on the passenger

seat of an electric cart while his master inspected the golf course. Cute, Danica might say. She sees the good in every mutt, mangy or not. Me? I'm immune to cute.

It was the last Tuesday morning in June. The sun glowed a buttery yellow behind a gray deck of early morning clouds. A thin mist hung between the oaks and maples that lined the dewy fairways. An earthy smell filled the air, a mix of turf and cut grass laced with the tangy aroma of fertilizer. In the distance, a lawn mower buzzed.

Tuesday was Ladies Day, which meant that the fifty-odd members of the Ladies Golf Association soon would arrive to play in the weekly shotgun tournament. I would be long gone by then, heading off to play in the sectional qualifying round for the U.S. Open. I shouldn't have been here at all, except Charlie asked me to open the shop and pull out a couple of dozen electric carts from the barn. I refused initially, citing my elaborate pre-tournament rituals, until Charlie reminded me of his generosity in allowing me practice time. So here I was, working my day job when I should have been soaking my joints in a warm bath.

The cart barn, like the greenskeeper's cottage, was a misnomer that evoked quaint but inaccurate images. The barn wasn't a freestanding red barn with a silo and hayloft, but a long, architecturally bland garage attached to the pro shop. It was dank and dark, perpetually abuzz with electric chargers juicing hundreds of cart batteries. The front part of the barn was a new addition. It had cinder-block walls and a peaked roof and was big enough to hold twenty carts with flimsy fiberglass sunroofs attached to their frames.

The back part, the original barn, had plywood walls and a roof that sloped so low, I needed to duck.

Duke nosed along the bottom of the barn door, where a strip of rubber touched the blacktop.

"Hey, Duke," I said. "Hey, boy."

I wasn't being friendly. I just didn't want to startle the mutt into nipping at my ankle. I jingled my keys for good measure.

Duke didn't react. He moved studiously along the bottom of the door, his nose leaving streaks of moisture on the rubber strip. Did a wet nose mean a dog was healthy or sick? I didn't know. Duke's breathing was loud and arrhythmic. A rasp here, a snort there. He reached the end of the door, whimpered, then sat back on his haunches and looked at me.

"What is it, boy?" I said. "Lose something?"

Danica must have been rubbing off on me. She spoke to dogs as if they were people, invested their every burp, twitch, and dumb expression with deep meaning. I felt ridiculous, not only asking Duke a question, but then staring into his rheumy eyes as if expecting an answer.

"Right," I muttered.

Opening the garage door was a two-handed job. I jammed the key into the lock and jiggled it with my right hand while twisting the door handle with my left. The handle resisted, gave a little, then resisted again before finally letting go.

"There," I said, feeling the thrill of a minor triumph.

The door was made of hinged wooden panels attached by tiny metal wheels to two grooved tracks. I usually yanked it up waist high, then adjusted my position to press it over my head like a weight lifter. Today, it stuck at about knee level, allowing Duke to scoot underneath. I wondered what he was up to, but not with any strong sense of curiosity. My real concern was lifting the door without pulling a muscle or pinching a nerve. The bottom right wheel stuck at a kink in the metal track. Someone, probably a caddie, must have rammed it with an electric cart. These accidents happened occasionally, and the usual remedy was a bang or two from a hammer. Duke snorted as I jiggled the wheel through the kink and pushed the door overhead. He was sniffing at something I couldn't quite make out in the dim middle of the barn. I slapped at the light switch and nearly choked.

Duke was sniffing at his master.

Rick Gilbert hung between two carts in a space created by a third cart pulled out of line. The rope—a clothesline tied in a typical hangman's noose—hooked over a rafter and angled down to another cart, where it was tied to the bumper. Rick wore his customary dark green overalls and pale yellow T-shirt. His head lay against his right shoulder, his tongue bulging thickly between his lips. His face was flushed, a deep red, almost purplish tinge bleeding through his dark tan.

Something between a groan and a cry escaped my lips and slowly faded into the background buzz of a single battery charger. The body suddenly started to rotate at the precise moment a seam opened in the clouds. Sunlight streamed into the yard and reflected an eerily milky glow into the barn. I broke toward the pro shop, flipped open my cell phone, and stabbed at 911.

"Poningo Police."

"I'm at Harbor Terrace Country Club," I said. "A man's hanging in the cart barn."

"Hanging?"

"From a noose," I said.

"Calm down, ma'am. What's your exact location?"

I described where the pro shop was in relation to the large stone castle clubhouse that was a town landmark.

"Wait right there. A patrol car is on the way."

I sat on one of the patio chairs and hugged myself as the dew chilled me through my golf shirt. In a split second, the pedestrian had changed into the surreal. I concentrated on the caddie yard: the metal rail embedded in three pillars of concrete where golfers leaned their bags; the stand of lilacs shading the benches where the caddies waited for their loops; the tin shack where Eddie-O kept the tee times and the cart keys and generally tried to impose order.

Beyond the lilacs, a stretch of parking lot narrowed to a tree-lined maintenance road that ran down to the lower holes near the water. The arborvitae wall began at the mouth of the road and circled the cottage where Rick Gilbert lived with his family. His wife and son were in the cottage now, sleeping most likely, unaware that Rick was hanging in the cart barn. Dead.

A loud bang startled me. Down below, a truck jounced off the first fairway and pulled itself onto the paved path climbing toward the yard. I quickly got up and ran to the barn. Studiously averting my eyes from Rick, I dragged down the door as far as the kink in the track just as the truck lumbered past. The driver, one of the greens crew I knew by sight but not by name, waved. A greens mower rattled in the truck bed.

I turned back to the patio. A short man dressed in kitchen whites stood by the table where I'd been sitting.

"*Buenos días, Señora Jenny,*" he said.

"Hello, Reynaldo." I hurried back to the chair.

Reynaldo worked in the clubhouse restaurant. I often saw him early in the morning, walking up from the apartments attached to the back of the cart barn.

"Is everything okay?" he said.

"Sure. Fine. No problem."

"Don't you take carts out?" he said. He was short and neat, kind of handsome, really, with a bandito mustache that interfered with the pleasing combination of angles and planes that made up his face. He always waited our table at the Tuesday afternoon luncheon. The girls and I tipped him generously, more generously than the service deserved, because we knew he sent every extra dollar back home to his family in Guatemala.

"I am. I will," I said. "Just not now."

"I help?"

"No, Reynaldo. Thanks. Don't you have your own job?" His early morning routine was to haul in the bread delivery, fire up the ovens, and generally get the kitchen ready for the day.

In the distance, a siren wailed. Reynaldo shrugged, shoved his hands into his pockets, and headed up the hill. He reached the clubhouse just as a patrol car rounded the circle and sped down. It stopped at the edge of the patio, its tires crunching a thin layer of sand spread on the blacktop.

The cop got out and ceremoniously fixed his hat on his head. He was tall and thin, with sharp features and a trimmed mustache.

"You call in the body?" he said, his eyelids narrowed into a squint barely wide enough to admit light.

"Yes, I . . ."

He walked past me and slowly circled the yard, jiggling the pro shop's doorknob, rapping his knuckles on the side of the tin shack, peering behind the lilacs. He came back and planted himself in front of me.

"Where is it?" he said.

He stood behind me as I lifted the barn door. I'd left on the lights, so there was no mistaking what was inside. The body now faced away from the door. Duke sat below, staring up as if waiting for his master's voice.

"Whose dog?" said the cop.

"His," I said.

The cop crouched near Duke and extended his hand, palm down. Duke sniffed the hand, then settled back into his vigil. The cop stood up, pushed his hat back on his head, and slowly walked around the body. He unclipped a tiny radio from his epaulet. Static crackled.

"Hennigsen, post twelve, over," he said.

"Go ahead, twelve."

"No mistake here. Got a hanger. Dead, too. Better send Donahue."

"Ten four."

Hennigsen clipped the radio and turned toward me.

"You didn't believe me," I said.

"Ma'am?"

"What you just said. You really didn't believe what I reported."

"Well, ma'am, it's been my experience that lots of reports coming from lay people aren't accurate."

"What was so wrong about this one?" I said. "I opened the door and found him."

"I accept that, ma'am." He spread his arms, shooing me back from the doorway. "You can tell your whole story to Detective Donahue."

"How long will that take? I have someplace I need to be."

"It'll take as long as Detective Donahue thinks it should take, ma'am. He'll be here in a few minutes. Meanwhile, I need to secure the area."

TWO

FOR HENNIGSEN, SECURING the area meant stringing yellow tape across the barn door and standing nearby with his arms folded across his chest. His radio crackled occasionally, but the calls were from other cops investigating other inaccurate reports from the town's fair citizenry. I was already feeling that rushed, wind-at-my-back tension of having lots to do and little time to do it. Sam was home asleep, and getting him going in the morning was like rousing a hibernating bear. I opened my cell phone in the fond hope I might wake him but closed it immediately as a car rounded the clubhouse circle, rolled down the slope, and tucked itself between Hennigsen's car and mine. It was a gray sedan, nondescript except for deeply tinted glass and a spotlight attached to the side mirror. A man got out. He scanned the yard with even more wary detachment than Hennigsen. His eyes swept across me, and I imagined myself appearing to him like a blip on a radar screen or a smudge on a heat sensor.

Detective Donahue—I assumed he was Detective Donahue—took off his suit jacket, folded it carefully, and laid it on the front seat of his car before heading to the barn. His white dress shirt still showed creases from the dry cleaner's box. Beneath it was a swimmer's body, wide shoulders tapering smartly to a narrow waist. He spoke briefly to Hennigsen, who pointed me out as someone he needed to question. Then they both ducked under the tape.

Three cars paraded into the parking lot and fanned out into three adjacent spaces midway down the hill. Three ladies got out of the cars and, rather than open their trunks and exchange street shoes for golf shoes, stood together and stared at the police cars. After a brief discussion, they moved in formation, circling wide to a point in the parking lot where they could see past the lilacs and into the barn. They froze there and raised their hands to their gaping mouths.

"Morning, ma'am." The detective stepped onto the patio. He had rolled up both his sleeves. Several plastic bracelets hung on his left wrist: yellow, light blue, pink, pale green. "I'm Detective Donahue."

"Jenny Chase," I said. I stood quickly, scraping the metal feet of the chair on the cement patio.

He was a head taller than me, and that head was squared off by close-cropped gray blond hair and etched, though not unpleasantly so, with deep lines around the mouth. He opened a small pad and scribbled my name with a ballpoint pen.

"Is that Miss, Ms., or Mrs.?" he said.

"Jenny," I said. "Just Jenny."

He looked up from the pad. He had the kind of blue eyes I'd read about only in trashy romance novels but never saw in real life.

"Well, Jenny, what were you doing here at such an early hour?"

"I'm the assistant pro. I was opening up for my boss."

My boss. I must have been more nervous than I thought. I never referred to Charlie as "my boss."

"And that is . . . ?"

"Charlie Bevridge. He's the golf pro."

Donahue looked over his shoulder. More cars had pulled into the lot, and the original three ladies had tripled to nine.

"Looks like you have some business," he said.

"It's Ladies Day," I said. "We have about fifty golfers every Tuesday morning."

"Excuse me."

Donahue went back to the barn, spoke to Hennigsen, then yanked down the barn door halfway.

"We don't need people gawking at him," he said when he returned. "Is there any place we can speak privately? I have some questions. They won't take long."

"I don't suppose there's much doubt what happened," I said.

"Maybe not, but I still need to investigate."

I unlocked the pro shop door. I must have opened the shop a hundred times in the last four summers and never once forgot to disable the burglar alarm. Until today. The door stuck in the humidity, and the moment I shouldered it open, the siren blared. I rushed inside, punched the code into the panel, then dialed the alarm company to report my mistake.

"Exciting," Donahue said.

He grinned, and I could see a twinkle in his eye. I felt myself flush.

Donahue looked around the shop, showing a nongolfer's amazement at the garish arrays of pastel outfits, two-toned golf shoes, putters, golf clubs, and golf bags. I sat on my stool, and he joined me at the counter.

"Let's start from the beginning," he said. "Tell me when you got here and what you found."

"I got here about seven," I said. "The golf course opens at eight on weekdays. On Tuesdays we have a shotgun tournament, so I need to pull out a bunch of electric carts."

"A shotgun?"

"A golf term. Sorry. It's a way of starting a tournament. We all begin on different holes, so we all finish at the same time. Then we have lunch on the clubhouse terrace."

Donahue scribbled some notes. "You keep saying 'we.' I thought you work here."

How far do I go into this? I wondered, and immediately decided not too far.

"I'm also a member of the club," I said, and shrugged to complete the thought.

"I see." Donahue flipped a page. "What did you find this morning?"

"It looked like a normal Tuesday when I drove in," I

said. "Except for Duke sniffing at the bottom of the barn door."

"That was odd?"

"He's Rick's dog, and he's usually with Rick. Rick is the greenskeeper. He inspects the course first thing every morning, and he borrows a cart to do that. Duke rides along with him."

"Before or after you get here?"

"Before."

"So he had a key to the barn," said Donahue.

"Right. He borrows the cart, rides the course, and returns it before I open up."

"What time would that be?"

"Whenever it gets light enough. He just needs to roll out of bed and walk over. He lives in the greenskeeper's cottage, right across the parking lot."

"Family?"

"Wife and son."

"Names?"

"The wife's name is Kit. The son is named Quint."

Donahue raised a hand. He was writing furiously but needed to catch up.

"Let's get to what you found," he said.

"Duke was sniffing at the door, and when I lifted the door he ran in. I had some trouble with the door."

"What kind of trouble?"

"Well, it's heavy. And somebody must have hit one of the tracks because the roller stuck. It happens pretty often. You get these caddies bombing around in electric carts. The barn was dark, so I didn't see Rick until I turned on the lights."

"The lights were off."

"Yes."

"And the door was locked or unlocked?"

"Locked."

"What did you do then?"

"I called nine one one and went outside to wait."

"The officer said he found the door down."

"I lowered it," I said. "I saw a maintenance truck heading in from the course. I didn't want any of the greens crew to see what happened."

Donahue stroked his chin. "Did you see anyone else around?"

"A restaurant worker named Reynaldo came by and asked if I needed help taking out the electric carts. I told him no, and he went away. That's when the officer drove in."

"What was he doing down here? The restaurant is up in the castle, right?"

"Yes, but there are some apartments behind the shop." I thumbed in the general direction. "He lives there."

"Is there another way into the barn from here?"

"I'll show you," I said.

A back door in the pro shop opened into the bag room, where the members stored their golf clubs. From the bag room, another door opened into the old part of the cart barn. Donahue followed me as I unlocked both doors.

"Thanks," he said, and dismissed me with a curt nod.

Back in the pro shop, I found Charlie standing near the counter. Charlie was portly but deceptively tall, with dark eyes, black hair going white along the margins, and a devilish goatee.

"Ladies outside said Rick Gilbert hung himself in the barn. Is that true?"

The morning suddenly caught up with me. I'm not a fainter, so I didn't recognize the wobbly feeling in my knees. I started to sink and missed my chance to catch myself on the counter. Somehow, without any perceptible movement, Charlie caught me under the arms. We hugged only on special occasions, and I usually deflected the ardor in his embrace by retreating into the cool, reserved college professor persona I still resurrected as needed. Today, I didn't care. I leaned hard against his firm belly and pressed my chin into his shoulder. He wore the best colognes, and this one evoked a mental image of being a girl again and flying Superman style over a landscape of rolling green hills.

I snapped myself out of it.

"Are you okay, Jen?"

I got my legs under me and pushed myself back.

"I think so," I said. "Just went wobbly for a moment."

Charlie let go. I fluffed my hair with my fingers.

"Wait a second," he said. "Did you . . . ?"

"Yeah, I found him." And I told Charlie exactly how.

"Holy shit," he said. "Who's in charge?"

"A detective named Donahue questioned me. He's in the barn."

"I want to talk to him," said Charlie.

I followed Charlie as far as the doorway from the bag room to the barn. More cops had arrived, along with two men wearing blue windbreakers with "ME" in large gold letters. Charlie deftly sliced Donahue off to the side, and within seconds the two men were chatting amiably. Charlie had qualities that were both endearing and infuriating, and one of the former was his ability to engage anyone in any type of situation, including a police detective in proximity to a dead body. It was hard to believe that Charlie was possibly the most disorganized person on the planet and that I spent my days trying to inject some order into his life.

Suddenly, the barn door flew up.

"Need you out here!" Hennigsen shouted.

Donahue immediately broke away from Charlie and hurried outside.

I went back through the pro shop and out to the patio. Kit Gilbert was slumped in a chair. Her eyes were closed and her arms dangled limply over the armrests. A few feet away, a teenage boy wearing cartoon pajamas sat Indian style. He rocked sideways, punctuating each movement by slamming his fist onto the concrete.

Donahue crouched in front of Kit.

"Mrs. Gilbert," he said gently. "Mrs. Gilbert, I'm George Donahue. I'm a police detective."

Kit Gilbert was a severely thin woman, lost in her simple pink housedress. Her mouse brown hair hung limply. Her hands were chafed, her fingernails chewed down to the nubs.

"Mrs. Gilbert," Donahue said again.

He patted one cheek, then the other. Kit's body stiffened. She opened her eyes, her gaze swirling and then fixing on Donahue.

"No!" she wailed.

The boy jumped onto Donahue's back, locking his arms around the detective's neck. Donahue's face quickly turned red, but he did not panic. He held firm, as if considering his next move, then expertly broke the boy's grip and reversed their positions.

"Quint, take it easy, son. . . . Easy." He spoke with genuine tenderness, as if he'd known the boy all his life.

The boy thrashed, then surrendered. Donahue whispered in the boy's ear as Hennigsen and another cop, acting on some signal I must have missed, slowly moved closer. Donahue removed one hand from his bear hug and began to rub Quint's back. The boy went as docile as a house cat; I almost could hear him purr. A few moments later, Donahue released him completely. The two cops walked him to Donahue's car and sat him behind the wheel.

Donahue returned to Kit Gilbert. She was wide awake now, hugging herself, her legs tightly crossed.

"Mrs. Gilbert, I'm sorry, but I need to ask . . ."

I felt myself go wobbly again. I wasn't quite sure why. But Charlie was close by, and I slipped my arm under his for support.

THREE

SAM SLOUCHED DEEP in the car seat. His spine bent at almost a right angle in a lumbar area not designed for such contortions. His bare knees pressed the door of the glove box. I hadn't seen his face since we backed out of the driveway. Two curtains of dark brown hair, still sopping from his shower, spilled from the cowlick above his forehead.

"You could have been ready," I said.

He tugged a couple of thin white wires. Two earbuds tumbled onto his chest.

"What?"

"I said, you could have been ready."

"You could have come home sooner."

"I couldn't. Something horrible happened at the club."

Sam shook the hair off his face. He had deep-set eyes and a perfectly straight nose and a jaw that was beginning to assert itself as his baby fat melted away. I often wondered if he had any idea of the effect he'd have on women some-day. But this wasn't one of those moments.

"I found Rick Gilbert hanging from a rafter in the cart barn."

"Hanging?" said Sam. "Like dead?"

"Hanging," I said. "And he actually was dead."

"Wow. Did you like scream?"

"I didn't. The sight was so stunning I was dumbstruck. I just backed out of the barn and called the police. That's why I couldn't get home sooner. A detective needed to question me."

"You mean you got like interrogated?"

"Way too strong a word." I thought of Detective Donahue and felt a silly grin try to form on my face. "It was more of a conversation."

"Rick was kinda weird," said Sam.

"How do you mean?" In Sam's lexicon, "weird" had subdefinitions that went on for pages.

"Just weird. All the caddies say so. They say he looks kind of funny at them."

"How do you mean funny?"

"You know." Sam contorted his face into a clownish grin. Then he pressed his earbuds back into place and lowered his head. The curtains closed on this conversation.

THIS YEAR'S SECTIONAL qualifying for the Women's U.S. Open was at the Westchester Country Club. I arrived later than I wanted, but not too late for my pre-round warm-ups. The day had turned hot and humid, with a hazy white sky that cast fuzzy, indistinct shadows. I loved this weather. If I couldn't play in the aftermath of a summer downpour, give me hazy, hot, and humid. My muscles reacted well in this climate, and halfway through my tub of balls on the practice range, I felt loose and lithe.

Westchester South was the easier of the club's two layouts, but the buzz along the practice range was that conditions were altered to U.S. Open specifications, with a five-inch rough and greens cut to the speed of glass. I finished off with half a dozen drives, then headed for the practice green. Cindy Garfield stood waiting for me on the fringe. She already knew about Rick, but not that I discovered him.

"My God, what a way to start the day," she said. She patted her chest, faking palpitations. "But then again, I wouldn't be too broken up to find Eric hanging in the basement."

Cindy wore a wide-brimmed straw hat and huge sunglasses. Her arms and legs glistened with coconut-scented sunscreen.

"You don't mean that," I said.

"Yes, I do," said Cindy. "You try sitting in that bookstore five days a week while he tells the same stories over and over. 'I once met John Updike on Fifth Avenue.' 'I once sat next to John Cheever on the train.'"

"I like his stories," I said. "I mean Eric's."

"But they aren't true. He never met John Updike. He never sat next to John Cheever on the train. The closest he ever got was sitting three seats behind someone he *thought* was John Cheever."

"He sells a lot of books," I said.

"Yes." Cindy sighed. "He sells a lot of books."

"And you throw great parties."

"Yes. I suppose we do." Cindy stroked her chin thoughtfully. "Of course, Eric never would commit suicide because he never would finish writing the suicide note. It would be so long, so filled with literary allusions, he never would get it quite right and would give up on the whole project."

Cindy was the handsomest woman I knew. She had precisely sharp features, a slim figure, and lush, prematurely silver hair. "I get quality points for looking older than my age," she was fond of saying. She and Eric owned the Garfield Reading Room, the last but still highly successful independent bookstore in our part of the county. They were an odd match: regal, reserved Cindy and anxious, balding, butterball-round Eric. Cindy felt about Eric the way most women felt about their husbands after a certain number of years: She was tired of his act. I hadn't gotten that far with Roger, but if I extrapolated our path from the fork where our lives diverged, I probably would have reached that same point by now.

I dropped three balls onto the green and smacked long lags at a distant hole. By the time I completed my circuit of the green, Stephanie Stein and Lulu Errico had joined Cindy. Steph and Lulu were sisters, short and buxom with dark hair and Mediterranean skin. Steph, divorced and well-off settlementwise, worked part-time as a medical receptionist and dabbled in different charitable causes. Lulu was a pre-school teacher and married to a lawyer who practiced in town. Together with Cindy, they were my steady playing partners in the Tuesday morning shotguns. And the three of them, together with Danica Ward, made up my inner circle of friends.

Cindy was telling them about Rick when I drew up.

"Jenny found him," she said. "Lifted the barn door, and there he was."

"Oh, my God!" Steph and Lulu said in unison.

I picked up from there, telling the story right up to Donahue's gentle handling of Quint Gilbert.

"What exactly is wrong with that boy?" said Steph.

"Autism," said Lulu.

"I thought it was more of a general mental retardation," said Cindy.

"No, it's autism," said Lulu. "He falls pretty far up the spectrum, too."

"How do you know?" said Cindy.

"The Autism Awareness Center," said Lulu. "It opened about a year ago, right around the block from your store. They use new approaches to connect these kids to the world. Like computers."

"A widow with an autistic son," said Steph. "What's going to happen to them?"

"They'll get thrown out of their house, for starters."

We all snapped our attention to Cindy.

"They live in the greenskeeper's cottage. The cottage comes with the job. No greenskeeper, no cottage. Jenny, if anyone knew that, I thought it would be you."

I did know that, I suppose. I just hadn't spent my morning following through on the ramifications of Rick Gilbert's death.

AN EVENT LIKE a U.S. Open qualifier is heavily contested but sparsely attended. As we drove off the first tee, our gallery consisted of the husband of one of my playing partners, the lover (I gathered) of the other, and my three friends. Throw in the three caddies, and you had the whole tribe.

I made pars on the first three holes, mainly because I kept the ball in the fairway. My two playing partners each found the deep rough once and on each occasion needed to scramble to make double bogey. The fourth hole was a short par three with an elevated tee and a pond angling across the right front corner of the green. My tee shot stuck two feet from the pin, and I canned the putt for a birdie. My fans applauded. I was one under par after four holes. This was going well.

I climbed the steps onto the next tee and surveyed the fairway. Sam set the bag down next to me.

"Isn't it great being out here?" I said. "You've got to admit that."

"Why?" said Sam. "Because you just made a birdie? I'm supposed to be happy?"

"You could be happy for your mother."

"I am. See?" He forced an artificial grin.

"You know, Sam, with your talent this game is yours for the asking."

Rather than answer, Sam shouldered my bag and followed the other caddies onto the wooden footbridge that crossed a deep gully between the tee and the crest of the hill where the fairway began. At the edge of the tee, Cindy frowned. She knew about my running argument with Sam and had picked up on the latest installment. I smiled to disarm her, then began my setup. I pressed my tee into the ground, stood behind the ball to pick a target out of the distant tree line, took my stance. I waggled the club three times and between each resighted the target. But something seemed wrong. My driver felt as light as a toothpick, and my target blended into the horizon.

"Sorry," I said, and stepped away.

I needed to reorient myself.

The summer after my twelfth birthday, my father allowed me to work in his shop. I instantly fell in love with the pastel colors of the clothes, the shiny silver of the clubs lined up on their display stands, the tinkle of the bell whenever the door opened, the thickened Cockney accent my father used when talking to customers. Occasionally, he would close the shop early and strap our bags to the back of an electric cart. His was a huge black-and-white leather kangaroo with his name stitched onto its belly. Mine was a thin canvas with seven mismatched clubs. He kept his preaching to a minimum as we played in the long shadows of the evening. I was a natural, he said. Articulating in words what my muscles already knew would just confuse me.

One evening toward the end of that summer, I scored a birdie on a short par three. I practically sprinted to the next tee, got into my stance, and prepared to whale away. My father stopped me.

"You are about to hit the toughest shot in golf," he said.

The fairway in front of me was wide and flat, no sand or water, barely a tree.

"This is like the easiest shot on the course," I said. Three years in America, and I had already lost my accent and picked up the slang.

"I'm talking about any tee shot after a birdie," he said. "You're excited, your muscles are gorged with blood. Your swing won't be your own. For this shot, you need to relax."

For years, I carried this lesson in my head. I'd make a birdie and set up to drive on the next tee, and a tiny homunculus of my father would pop on my shoulder and whisper into my ear. But the specific image had faded, folded itself into my subconscious. Why I thought of it now, I didn't know.

Cindy caught my eye and silently asked if I was okay. I nodded. I was. I relaxed my arms, let my shoulders go limp. When I set up again, the weight was back in the club head and my target on the horizon shone like a beacon. I swung. The ball whistled across the gully, paused at the height of its trajectory, and then drifted down.

"Thanks, Dad," I whispered as I lifted my tee from the turf.

FOUR GOLFERS OUT of the field of 120 qualified. My two under par 70 was the lowest score. No one else was close.

The local cable channel interviewed me beside the eighteenth green. Charlie treated himself to a congratulatory bear hug when I got back to the club, and the Ladies Golf Association pinned a computer-generated banner across the bulletin board on the pro shop patio. But as I'd come to expect in my adult life, the sense of triumph faded once I returned home. Dinner and dishes, mail and bills, the stress over whatever Sam might plan for the night.

At least this last bit of stress was removed from me: Sam plopped himself in the beanbag in the den and played video games all night. Cindy begged off my standing invitation for a glass of wine on the screened-in porch. I poured myself a glass of Pinot Grigio and sat on the porch by myself, trying to wrap my mind around how the discovery of a dead body might have presaged what could be the most important round of golf I ever played. I didn't get too far. In fact, I didn't even finish the wine before a powerful fatigue overcame me.

I was halfway up the stairs when Sam called. There was something I needed to see.

"Show me later," I said, expecting it was a new high score in some lurid fantasy world.

"Come now," he said.

Sighing, I headed down to the den and found Sam had the TV tuned to the national golf cable channel. My face filled the screen.

"They've been running it all day. I forgot to tell you."

All day? I wondered if . . . perhaps . . . maybe . . .

"I'm going up, Sam. Not too late."

"I'll be up in a minute. I'm tired, too."

My father paid intense attention to every little event in the world of golf. He prided himself on being connected, on being in the know, on cobbling together bits of info he could transmute into business opportunity gold. I imagined that one source of his knowledge was the national golf cable channel, and I thought that maybe, possibly, he had seen my interview.

I sat on my bed and lifted the answering machine. No messages. Disappointed, but not completely, I turned to the caller ID. I'd bought the combination phone, answering machine, and caller ID during the winter but had stopped ticking through the call log at the end of the day after the novelty of seeing how many telemarketers had called wore off.

I pressed the button, displaying the recent calls in reverse order. Telemarketer, Charlie, telemarketer, Cindy. Then came five calls, all in a row and all from the same unidentified number. The calls had come early last evening—I had been food shopping, I remembered—and the caller hadn't left a message.

"Sam," I called, "can you come in here?"

Surprisingly, Sam materialized at my door within seconds. His pajamas consisted of oversize basketball shorts and an even more oversize skateboarding T-shirt.

"Does this number look familiar?" I showed him the screen.

"Nope." He yawned. "I'm off to bed. G'night."

"Good night, Sam." I found a patch of forehead and kissed it. "Sleep well."

I normally don't return calls to strange, unidentified numbers. But the possibility that this one could have been my father calling to wish me luck in the qualifier was too tempting to resist. I picked up the phone and pressed the send button.

The call connected after the second ring. No one spoke. All I could hear was the hollow sound of an open line and, perhaps, the *whoosh* of a fan.

"Who's this?" I finally said.

"Who's *this*?" responded a man's voice.

"Jenny."

"Did you say Danny?"

"No. Jenny."

"Jenny Chase from Harbor Terrace Country Club?"

"Yes. Dad?"

"I'm not your dad. Where are you?"

"I'm home," I said, immediately regretting my answer. Who was this guy?

Papers rustled in the background.

"This is Detective Donahue. I'll be right over."

FOUR

WITHIN FIVE MINUTES, a gray sedan rolled up in front of the house. I waited at the door, watching through the screen while tiny moths flitted around the two carriage lights. Donahue popped out of the car. He stood for a moment and rubbed his eyes before leaning in to grab his suit jacket. He slipped into the jacket as he walked up the flagstone path. Every movement suggested that this had been a long day.

"Ms. Chase," he said.

"Detective Donahue," I said.

I pushed open the screen just enough for him to squeeze through. A moth rode in on his shoulder, but I expertly flicked it back into the night. Donahue straightened his jacket and cleared his throat. His eyes looked sleepy.

"I need to know why you called that number," he said.

"I need to know what your number was doing on my caller ID."

"It isn't my number."

"Whose is it?"

"I'm asking the questions," he said.

My last image of Donahue was of his gentle handling of Quint Gilbert. His sharp tone surprised me.

"I saw a strange number when I checked my caller ID log, so I called back."

"Do you always call back a strange number when you see one?"

"No. Not usually."

"But sometimes?"

"Actually I never have."

"So why tonight?"

"It's a long story," I said.

He glanced at his watch. "Shorten it."

"I qualified for the U.S. Open today. That may not mean anything to a nongolfer, but it's a big deal to me. Anyway, I thought my father may have seen the results, so I checked my answering machine to see if he called to congratulate me. He didn't, so then I checked caller ID to see if he called without leaving any message. I saw the strange number and thought it might have been him."

"Show me," said Donahue.

I led him up the stairs. As I passed Sam's bedroom, I stopped and pushed open the door. Sam lay in bed, his face lit by the glow of a portable DVD player.

"Sam," I called, then more forcefully, "Sam!"

Sam plucked an earbud from one ear. "What?"

"This is Detective Donahue," I said. Sam could see him in the doorway. "He's here to ask me some questions. Not much longer with the video."

Sam groaned and pressed the bud back into his ear.

"Do you have teenagers?" I asked Donahue.

"One."

"Then you can understand."

Donahue said nothing. He was a police detective. His teenager probably was as obedient as a Marine recruit.

In the bedroom, Donahue stood at a respectful distance while I sat on the bed and ticked through the caller ID log in reverse. The last call had come at 10:05 P.M., the first at 8:30 P.M. I waved Donahue over and went through them again.

"You didn't tell me there were five calls," he said.

I shrugged.

"You didn't answer any of them?"

"I wasn't home."

"What about Sam?"

"He never answers the land line. His friends call him on his cell."

"You checked the log tonight, but not last night?"

"I use it for screening calls, not logging them. I had no reason to check last night."

"Do you carry a cell phone?"

"Yes," I said.

"Any calls from that number on your cell?"

"No. I would have seen those."

"I want to look at those calls one more time."

I pressed the button while Donahue recorded the time of each call in his little spiral notebook.

"First off, you know those calls didn't come from me. They came from a cell phone." He paused. "Rick Gilbert's cell phone."

For the third time today, I felt myself go wobbly in the knees. I quickly sat on the bed.

"Why would Rick Gilbert call me?"

"That's what I want to know. How well did you know him?"

"The way I know many people at the club. Casually. Some days I see him, some days I don't. Some days we say hi to each other, some days we don't."

"How long did he work there?"

"About fifteen years."

"And you?"

"This is my fourth summer working, but I've been a member for seventeen years."

"And during all that time, Rick Gilbert never called you?"

"No," I said. "Maybe."

"What does that mean?"

"My ex-husband, Roger, was very involved with the club. Sat on committees, served on the board of directors. There could have been times Rick called Roger to discuss club business."

"But you don't know that for a fact."

"No."

"Has Roger been out of the picture long?"

"Four years."

"And Rick would have known that?" said Donahue.

"I don't know what Rick would have known. But Roger

hasn't been involved in the club for four years. Rick would have known that."

Donahue twisted his mouth and bit his lower lip as if lost in thought. A hint of blond stubble had risen on his jawline since morning, not that I was paying close attention.

"What do you think this all means?" I said.

"Probably nothing," said Donahue.

"Wait a second. I get five calls in one night from a man I hardly speak to, he kills himself the next morning, you rush over here to investigate this, and now you say it probably means nothing?"

"The clearest thing in the world is that Rick Gilbert hung himself this morning," said Donahue. "Even the clearest cases don't always tie up as neatly as we like. There always are loose ends, but most of them don't mean anything significant."

"And if you don't ever find out?"

"Life goes on, Jenny. It always does."

He pocketed his notebook, signaling that the interview was over. I led him to the stairs, noticing on the way that Sam's DVD player was off and that Sam's head was buried beneath a pillow.

"When I opened the barn door," I said as we descended the stairs, "the light was off."

"You told me."

"I did?"

"It's in my notes." He patted his pocket.

"Wouldn't it have been too dark in there for him to hang himself?"

"I tested the light with the door closed," he said. "There

are three air vents in the peaks of the roof. They let in a good amount of ambient light."

"So that's another insignificant loose end," I said.

"Right."

We reached the front door.

"Is there any chance Rick didn't kill himself?" I said.

Donahue paused with his hand on the screen.

"There's always a chance things are not what they seem," he said. "But I doubt that's the case here."

"What if I find out why he called me last night?"

He handed me a card. "Let me know."

He opened the screen and slipped through, careful not to let in any moths.

FIVE

THE NEXT TWO days marked a steady return to normalcy, both at the club and in my life. Golfers played and caddies caddied. Mowers buzzed the greens, trucks laden with fertilizer crisscrossed the fairways, sprinklers erupted from the turf with clockwork precision. Meanwhile, I descended from the twin highs of qualifying for the Open and seeing my face splashed across the national golf cable channel. The Open was several weeks away, and it would take some planning to make sure my game and my psyche peaked at the right time.

Friday morning, I found the yard already in high gear. Two rows of carts lined the green patch, the flaps of the starter shack were open, and several bodies lounged on the benches beneath the lilacs. I rolled down the hill and caught Charlie midway between the patch and the barn door. He wore black pants, a black sport jacket, and a white dress shirt open at the collar.

"Funeral's today," he said.

"I thought the services were private."

"Semi. Family, club officials, and club employees. We're all going."

"We are?" I said. "Who's minding the store?"

"No one. I'm closing the shop. Eddie-O is leaving the shack open. Anyone who wants to play is on the honor system."

"But I'm not dressed for it." I was in my basic nongolfing outfit: gray slacks and white polo shirt.

"You look fine," said Charlie. He tossed me a cart key. "Help me here. I want to take out an extra dozen. That should hold them until we get back."

GRAY'S FUNERAL HOME was a clapboard Colonial with green shutters and a white picket fence near the center of town. The three of us, including Eddie-O, drove there in Charlie's car.

"You got a small fortune in deposit cans back here," said Eddie-O. He had shaggy red hair and a walrus mustache. Sunken cheeks gave him an older, more wizened look than his forty years.

"Find a place for this one," said Charlie. He unstuck a Coke can from the dashboard cup holder and tossed it back.

A large parlor with its thermostat jacked up higher than it needed to be easily swallowed the thirty or so mourners. I spotted the club's board of directors, various committee chairpersons, and half the greens crew. The family filled the small front row. Kit and Quint sat beside each other,

Kit in a stiff black jumper and Quint in chinos and a blue blazer. His hair was raked sideways, slick with hair tonic, and he pressed a handheld computer game with his thumbs. An elegant blond woman at Kit's elbow looked as if she could have been her sister. The squat, ruddy man transfixed by Quint's game could have been Rick's brother.

I drifted away from Charlie and Eddie-O. Charlie, ever the politician, began schmoozing with the board while Eddie-O traded gibes with the greens crew. The casket was open and, former Catholic school girl that I was, I felt compelled to say a prayer.

Some people looked "good" in death, others looked terrible. Rick Gilbert was somewhere in the middle. The high color was gone from his face, leaving a pale cast to his skin. A yellow turtleneck covered what I expected to be rope burns. One eyelid wasn't completely closed, and a sudden gleam from within unsettled me. I cut short my prayer and pushed myself off the kneeler.

Quint and the uncle had gone somewhere, leaving Kit and her sister. They whispered to each other but looked up when I approached. I introduced myself to the sister, whose name was Jackie, then took Kit's hands and told her I was sorry.

"I know," she said. "Thank you."

We said nothing else, and after an awkward moment I backed away.

Along the side wall, two boards of family photographs stood on easels. There were shots of Rick and the infant Quint, Rick driving an ancient tractor, Rick and Kit dancing, Rick and Kit with Quint between them sitting on the steps of the greenskeeper's cottage. One photo, the largest of the lot, showed Kit and Rick in a sunny clearing among tall trees. Rick wore a powder blue tuxedo with wide lapels trimmed with black piping and a white ruffled shirt. His hair, redder and curlier than in his latter days, was picked into a huge Afro. Kit wore a simple white gown. Her hair was parted in the middle and pleated into two long braids. Tiny granny glasses rode low on her nose.

"Their wedding day," a voice said in my ear.

I moved over, and Jackie stepped beside me.

"Really?" I said. I took it to be a prom picture, Kit going with her much older boyfriend. "She looks like a child bride."

"No, they were the same age," said Jackie. "We've both been blessed with strong, slow-aging genes. Unfortunately, Kit's are no match for the stress in her life."

I followed her gaze back to Kit, who was speaking to the funeral director.

"They met in college. Lived together for two years. Got married the day after graduation. In the woods. Oh, they were quite the hippies back then." Jackie handled the word delicately, as if it were an object she needed to toss into the trash.

"How is she holding up?" I said.

"She's tough. I just don't know if she's as tough as she thinks she is. I've offered to have her come live with me. We have the room, but Kit won't hear of it."

"Maybe after everything settles down."

"As if it ever will," said Jackie. "Quint's services are the problem. Here she drives him two miles to a school with a special program. Up where we are, near Bennington, she would be driving forty-five."

"I can't imagine how difficult raising Quint must be," I said.

"No, you can't. Neither can I, for that matter, and I've seen some of it up close and personal when they visit."

The funeral director tapped a finger on the microphone, raising a whine of feedback. Charlie and Eddie-O took seats in the last row. I broke away to join them, but Jackie grabbed my arm.

"She doesn't believe what happened," she said.

"I suppose it's like landing on another planet."

"I mean that literally," she whispered. "She doesn't believe Rick killed himself."

I was about to mention the phone calls, then thought better.

"Well, I'm sure—"

"You found him. What do you think?"

"He was hanging," I said.

"But how? It was in a garage, Kit told me. How could he have done it where he did it?"

"I'm no expert," I said.

Jackie dropped my arm and walked away.

The funeral director led everyone in a short prayer, then gave way to the chairman of the greens committee. The chairman spoke about the great job Rick had done and how his years of experience and store of local knowledge would be sorely missed. He then digressed into a technical summary of how Rick prevented a virulent weed from taking over the golf course some years back.

"It nearly cost him," the chairman said dramatically, and sat down.

Rick's brother spoke briefly about their boyhood in Vermont. He told a story about a vacant lot near their home and how one summer Rick transformed it into a scaled-down version of a real golf course. He told how excited Rick had been to land his first real job after college as assistant greenskeeper at Congressional outside Washington. He spoke of how proud Rick had been to be the head greenskeeper at Harbor Terrace and how he often said he never wanted to work anywhere else.

"We must be careful what we wish for," he added dryly.

In conclusion, he unfolded a piece of yellow construction paper with purple crayon scribblings.

"I don't know if you can see this," he said. "It says, 'I'll miss you, Daddy. Quint.'"

I heard sobbing from the front row. Kit slumped against her sister, her shoulders quivering. My eyes welled up. I've attended many funerals, too many, in fact, and usually play to my reputation as the stiff, reserved Brit. But the tears come on occasion, and when they do, they come less from within me than from some reaction to another's expression of grief. Quint's simple, innocent note got me.

Charlie patted my hand, then took it in his. I let it stay.

The funeral director closed with a few prayers. Outside, we all lined the side street in idling autos, waiting for the funeral procession to begin. A pallbearer came down the line, sticking magnetized purple flags on each hood.

"Hey, Charlie," Eddie-O said after the man passed. "You got a couple of these flags buried back here."

Charlie shrugged, then caught my eye. He had vulpine features but could summon a particular sheepish grin I found irresistible.

The Greenwood Cemetery was pastoral in a way that few cemeteries were anymore. The trees grew tall and thick and cast substantial tracts of shade. The land rolled, the hills offering vantage points, the dales creating tiny amphitheaters of privacy. A creek twisted through, at one point spreading into a pond where, on a morning as calm as this one, a pair of swans skimmed a surface as smooth as slate.

The procession stopped on a stretch of road that curved around the base of a hill. There was a long wait while the pallbearers staged the casket at the grave site. Charlie rubbed his eyes. Eddie-O hoarsely whistled a fractured version of a funeral dirge. None of us had anything to say.

A signal to get out rolled down the line. Doors opened and slammed. A pallbearer distributed single roses as we gathered on the slope around the casket. The director conducted the service, reading from a book of prayers.

Off to one side, set away from the main group, stood a group of teenage boys surrounded by adults. The boys had been dressed exactly like Quint in chinos and blazers, and together they might have resembled a prep school choir. But by now several ties hung loose and many shirttails flew. Some stood with their hands jammed in their pockets. Others fidgeted. Two shoved each other until an adult intervened. Off to the other side, a gray sedan bumped off the road and onto the grass. The door opened, and Detective Donahue slowly unfolded himself. He stood at attention beside the car, his eyes shaded by sunglasses.

The service ended, and the director invited us to pay our last respects. Charlie and I pressed closer. In the distance, I heard a door slam and an engine ignite. When I turned back from tossing my rose onto the casket, Donahue was gone.

Walking back to the car, I drew Charlie out of Eddie-O's earshot.

"Kit's sister spoke to me," I said. "She says Kit doesn't believe Rick killed himself."

"Does she have any reason?"

"No, but . . ." I waited for two of the greens committee to pass. "Did Rick ever ring you up?"

"Do you mean on the phone or on a cash register?"

"Phone, silly." Sometimes talking to Charlie was like talking to Sam, minus the attitude.

"He did on occasion," he said.

"What did you talk about?"

"Mostly my opinion about changes he wanted to make on the golf course."

"Did he call you at home or at the shop?"

"The shop," he said.

"Did he ever call you at home?"

"He could have. I don't remember. Why are you asking me about this?"

"Because Rick called me the night before he died. Not once, not twice. Five times."

"What about?"

"I don't know. I didn't talk to him."

"Do the cops know?"

"The cops are how I found out." I quickly explained

finding the number on the log, calling it, and getting Detective Donahue.

"Can you tell me, Jenny, why did you call that number at all?"

"I thought it could be my father."

"Oh," said Charlie. He knew the background and deftly changed the subject. "I was impressed by Donahue. What did he think?"

"Not much. He wrote down the times Rick called, then said it probably was an insignificant loose end. Tell you the truth, I don't know why he even came over."

"Maybe it wasn't about Rick."

"Charlie."

He grinned his sheepish grin.

We reached his car. Eddie-O already was sitting in the backseat. The hearse and limousine were gone. The other cars were starting up and driving away.

"Is this bothering you?" said Charlie. The grin was gone.

"Wouldn't it bother you? I was going to tell Kit's sister, then didn't think I should," I said.

I looked back at the deserted grave site. Several of the single roses had slipped off the casket and lay forlornly on the mantle of fake grass.

"Should I keep an extra close eye on you these next few days?" said Charlie.

I gave him my best Cheshire cat smile, the one I knew worked on him the way his sheepish grin worked on me.

"Charlie, I just qualified for the U.S. Open. Do you think I'd let anything get in my way?"

"I know you, Jenny. That's why I ask."

SIX

SATURDAY MORNING AT six-thirty, I stood listening at the bottom of the stairs while Sam performed his morning ablutions: a spurt of water to dampen his face; a second spurt followed by half a dozen strokes of a toothbrush; guttural groans as he dragged a comb through the knots in his hair. Finally came a visual: Sam hunkered down on the top step, peeling off his dirty socks and pulling on clean ones. Then he examined his sneakers like a South Seas islander encountering a laptop.

The morning was hectic, even for a Saturday. We moved a lot of merchandise, which was my least favorite aspect of the club professional job because I didn't believe that the kind of ball you hit, clubs you swung, or shoes you laced onto your feet made a damn bit of difference in how you played the game.

"Fake it," said Charlie, who had a vested interest in the membership's product preferences.

And I did, or at least tried to, because I wanted Charlie's shop to succeed. But anyone with the least bit of perspicacity could see that I was better at using inventory than hawking it.

At eleven, I emerged into a nearly deserted yard. Eddie-O, standing in the tin shack, dusted his hands in mock accomplishment.

"He's out," Eddie-O called.

The main cart path curved around the twelfth green and ended at the first tee about a hundred yards away. Several carts were parked at skewed angles, and the golfers stood in small groups. The caddies, each wearing a green bib with "HTCC" lettered in yellow, gathered in the shade of the oak tree about fifty yards forward of the tee. I spotted Sam's distinctive slouch.

"Who does he have?" I said, crossing to the shack.

"Judge Chandler."

Henry Chandler was one of two lawyers who shared the town's judicial duties as part-time judges. He had a reputation for not liking long-haired kids, either in his courtroom or out. Sam's hair, combined with this morning's attitude, did not bode well. The thought must have manifested itself on my face.

"Don't worry," said Eddie-O. "Sam's a good caddie. He'll be fine."

Shortly before noon, a special delivery package arrived for me. The thick cardboard envelope contained my U.S.

Open players credentials, parking pass, important contestant information, and a welcome package for the Charleston, West Virginia, area. I spread the stuff on the counter and leafed through it.

"This is really happening," I said.

Charlie nodded. He opened a drawer beneath the counter and handed me a shop stationery envelope wrapped with a sloppily tied pink ribbon.

"Open it," he said.

Inside was a printout of a motel reservation for two outside Charleston.

"Charlie, I—"

"One less thing for you to deal with," he said. "I heard all the players stay there."

"I don't know what to say."

"Don't say anything."

"But you did this . . . out of your own pocket."

"I didn't do it. A caddie helped me. And it's not my own pocket. It's the shop's."

"That's ridiculous." The shop's bank account and Charlie's pockets were one.

"It's not every day one of my staff qualifies for a major championship. Just say thank you."

I realized I was acting unfairly. I pecked his cheek and whispered, "Thank you," into his ear.

During the middle of the day, Charlie and I alternated giving lessons in half-hour blocks. We charged for lessons at the rate of $60 per half hour, and one-third of my fee went to Charlie under a rate structure established by the Professional Golfers Association, the umbrella group to which we both belonged. When Charlie first hired me, most of my pupils were young men who, I believed, were less interested in swing mechanics than in the possibility of sex with the teacher. Gradually, the novelty of a female assistant pro wore off, and my current crop of steady pupils was divided equally between women and young boys whose parents thought they would respond better to a maternal figure.

It was three-thirty when I finally came off the practice tee and sat down to the lettuce sandwich I'd brought for lunch. Sharp voices erupted in the yard, but I wasn't about to let the commotion interrupt me. Then the phone rang, the insistent double ring that identified it as a call from an internal number. I threw down my napkin, swallowed a bit of lettuce, and answered.

"Jen, Eddie. Better come out here."

This was the scene I walked into: Judge Chandler and Sam stood on opposite sides of the tin shack. Judge Chandler was a big, fleshy man with tiny glasses, thin blond hair, and patches of sweat darkening his light blue shirt. Sam had his caddie bib balled up in his fist, muddy streaks on his shorts, and dried grass crusting his sneakers.

They shouted at each other, trading accusations and denials. Eddie-O stood between them, arms extended, and tried to keep what little peace was left.

"Here she is," yelled Eddie.

The Judge turned toward me and, pointing dramatically through Eddie-O to Sam, thundered, "That boy is a thief!"

"I am not!" Sam shouted, and then added under his breath, "Dork-head."

"Quiet!" I screamed, and slammed the counter.

The impact rippled around the tin skin of the shack, converged at a focal point in the center, and exploded outward. Everyone fell silent.

Trying to appear judicious, I ignored both my son and the Judge and addressed Eddie-O. "What happened?"

"Well . . . ," said Eddie-O.

"That boy," the Judge cut in, "stole thirty dollars from me."

"The hell I did," said Sam.

"One at a time," I said. "Sam, let me hear what the Judge has to say first. Okay?"

Sam kicked the side of the shack. Another rumble coursed through the tin.

"This is my wallet," said Judge Chandler. He walked toward the bag rail, dredging his wallet from his pants pocket as he went. "This is my golf bag."

He patted a brown leather golf bag. Towels hung like theater curtains from the strap ring. Fanciful animal head covers, the shop's current loss leaders, stared cockeyed at the sky.

"When I play, I keep my wallet here." The Judge ripped the zipper of a pocket at the bottom of the bag. "I also segregate the money I plan to pay my caddie from the rest of my cash." He opened the wallet. "I fold that neatly in fourths and tuck it right here, behind this credit card. Today, after the round, I took my wallet from the bag. The money was gone."

"I didn't take it," said Sam.

I raised a hand.

"Geez, can't I even talk?"

"You'll have your chance." I focused back on the Judge. "Was the rest of your money there?"

"Yes. That wasn't touched."

"Maybe you didn't segregate your money today. Maybe you only thought you did."

"I do it before every round without fail," said the Judge. "And I distinctly remember doing it today because I needed to decide whether to segregate three tens or a ten and a twenty. I chose three tens."

"I don't have them. Look." Sam inverted the pockets of his shorts, spilling coins onto the pavement. Then he un-buttoned his shorts, dropped them, and pirouetted in his plaid boxers.

"That's enough, Sam," I said.

He buttoned his shorts, picked up a few coins, then kicked the rest of them away.

"I didn't see the money," I told the Judge.

"What does that prove? He was in possession of my golf bag, and therefore my wallet, for the last four hours. It's a cut-and-dried circumstantial case."

"Why would I take the money?" said Sam. "You were going to give it to me anyway."

"I don't pretend to understand the criminal mind," said the Judge.

"Enough with the criminal mind stuff," I said. "Sam, besides just denying this, can you explain why the Judge's money is missing?"

"Kieran took it," he said.

"The other caddie in the foursome," Eddie-O added helpfully.

"Where is he?" I said.

"He left," said Eddie-O.

"That's convenient," said the Judge.

I looked at Sam. "Do you really think Kieran took the money?"

Sam dragged a sneaker on the pavement. "Could have," he mumbled.

"This is getting nowhere," said the Judge. "I would be within my rights to call the police and press charges for petit larceny."

"And I would be within my rights to hire my son a lawyer and put a stop to this inquisition," I said.

"What do you propose?" said the Judge.

"You're out thirty dollars, but it's the same thirty dollars you would have paid Sam anyway. If Sam took the money, it was a stupid thing, granted, but he's not one penny ahead of where he would have been. If Sam didn't take the money, if this Kieran did, then Sam's out the thirty, too, and that's a lesson for both of you."

"I don't need lessons, but I need to leave," said the Judge. He turned to Sam. "Let me give you fair warning, young man. I have a long memory. And if I ever find you in my courtroom . . . well, let's just say never let me find you in my courtroom."

He walked through the yard and into the parking lot.

I looked at Eddie-O. He arched his eyebrows, and involuntarily, I arched mine back.

"Sam," I said, "what really happened?"

"I don't want to talk about it," he said.

"Sam, I need to—"

"No!" He flung himself away from the shack and ran around the cart barn to the snack bar.

Eddie-O sighed. "Hate to tell you this, Jen, but the Judge just made a formal complaint, which means I gotta suspend Sam."

"You mean he can't caddy?"

"No loops, no shagging on the practice tee, no hanging around the yard. Rules."

"Great," I said. "How long?"

"A week, unless the board tells me different."

"Goddammit," I muttered, and went back into the shop.

Charlie stood behind the counter, trying to complete the sale of a ridiculously expensive driver forged out of an exotic metal from deep in the periodic table. For some reason—Charlie's innocent explanation—the new touch-screen cash register wouldn't compute the advertised discount or accept the customer's credit card. I elbowed Charlie aside and completed the sale.

After the customer departed, I told Charlie about Sam and Judge Chandler. He listened sympathetically and groaned at each additional detail.

"Kieran Boyle," said Charlie. "Now there's a kid I wouldn't trust."

"Do you think he took the Judge's money?"

"Put it this way. If the Judge's money was stolen, and you stood Sam and Kieran side by side, I know who I would suspect."

The phone double rang. Charlie picked up, then handed me the receiver. It was Eddie-O.

"Sam wanted me to tell you he's leaving," he said.

"How's he getting home?" It was over two miles.

"Walking. I can see him way down past the twelfth tee, hopping the wall to the road. He told me to tell you he was going to lock himself in the house so nothing else bad could happen to him today."

SEVEN

I WANTED TO keep the evening light and breezy. No talk of the club, Judge Chandler, or the suspension. I grilled burgers on the patio; Sam scooted back and forth on his skateboard, the wheels click-clacking on the flagstones, his face a mask of deep, dissatisfied concentration. He parked in the corner and positioned himself on the board with both heels hanging over the side edge. He bent deeply at the knees, then jumped. Both he and the board flew into the air. The board spun lengthwise, landing on its wheels with a crisp click-clack. Sam landed a millisecond later, perfectly centered on the board.

"Nice," I said. "What's it called?"

"Kick flip," said Sam.

"Kick flip, huh?" I said. Most of the skateboard tricks Sam talked about had names that made no sense: Ollies, shove-its, pop shove-its. This one at least described the motion of the board.

I slid the burgers onto their buns and carried them onto the porch. Sam performed three more kick flips in rapid succession, then came inside and sat down. He looked about as happy as he would washing the dishes.

"That's some trick," I said.

He took a huge bite from the burger and talked around it.

"I'm working on a jumping kick flip. That's when you fly off a jump and do the kick flip in the air and land on your wheels and keep going."

"I had no idea you were so good."

"Yeah, well, maybe if you watched me," he said. "Maybe if you weren't always shoving golf in my face, maybe you would know something about my life."

"Is that how you see it?" I said. "That I shove golf in your face? I'm sorry. Golf is what I do, what your grandfather does, what you can do, too, because you have the natural talent."

Sam dropped his burger and wiped his mouth with a napkin. He wasn't yet nasty enough to fling himself away from the table, but I could see he wasn't far from that stage of our relationship.

"You know, Sam, I had this game, and then I let myself be talked out of it. But now I have it again and I won't let go. Sorry. That's my story. I don't want you to make the same mistake I made. I want you to follow your heart."

"You tell me to follow my heart," he said, "but you really want me to follow yours."

"And what does your heart tell you?" I said.

"I want to skateboard. I want to be a skateboard pro. They have them, you know."

"I know," I said. "I can't deny that. But do you understand how proud your grandfather would be if you took up golf, I mean really threw yourself into the game?"

"Yeah, yeah." Sam ripped at the burger and chewed it down. "And why do you always call him 'your grandfather'? Why don't you call him 'my dad'? He's your father."

"It's complicated," I said.

We finished dinner quickly and in silence. Sam cleared the table. I rinsed the dishes and silverware and loaded them into the dishwasher. By the time I finished, Sam was in the den, nested in his beanbag chair and entranced by a video game.

"Do you have any plans for the night?" I said.

"No."

"Want to invite someone over?"

Sam paused the game. "Aren't I like punished or grounded or something?"

"Your punishment is your suspension. That's enough of a lesson."

"Yeah, yeah. Always a lesson in things."

He re-engaged the game.

I withdrew from the den. Despite our tiff, I was relieved that Sam was staying home alone tonight. He was at the age when suburban kids began to experiment with alcohol, drugs, sex, and permutations of the three. I gave Sam his freedom because freedom ultimately was a building block of trust, and I tried to keep reasonable tabs on his adventures by calling him several times each night on his cell phone. I hadn't detected anything sinister yet. He hadn't come home giddy or stinking of beer or mysteriously and insatiably hungry. But these bad things loomed out there in the big world beyond the edge of the backyard, and to keep them at bay for one more night was a luxury that wouldn't last forever.

The doorbell rang, and a polite moment later Cindy marched in with an open bottle of Chardonnay.

"I'm sorry. I had to come down here," she said. She lived four houses up the street.

"I'm glad you did," I said.

"All Eric wants to do lately on a Saturday night is sit on the porch and do the Sunday *Times* crossword," she said. "'Isn't this great?' he says. Yeah, great. I feel like canceling home delivery so he'll need to wait till Sunday morning to buy the damn thing."

I poured two glasses, and we went out to the porch. A pair of big old musty chairs angled toward each other from either side of a glass-paneled lawyer's bookcase, a minor victory in my war with Roger. Cindy kicked off her sandals and tucked her feet under her.

"Do you ever miss it?" she said, staring at the spines of the books behind the glass.

"No," I said.

"You did it for ten years and you don't miss it even this much?" She pressed her thumb and forefinger together.

"A little," I said. "Sometimes. Like in the winter when Charlie is in Florida and I'm alone in the shop. I'll think about crunching across campus with my books under my arms and walking into a classroom to find the kids sitting around the table. That did excite me."

"*Nothing Like the Sun?*" Cindy turned her head sideways and reared back to focus.

"A novel about Shakespeare by Anthony Burgess," I said. "I used it in a course called 'Shakespeare for Scientists.' Eric actually ordered it for me. He knew all about it."

Cindy rolled her eyes and slugged some Chardonnay. "How's the practicing going?" she said.

"It isn't yet. My game moves in a sine curve. I peaked at the qualifier and I need to go through the trough well before the Open."

"I heard about Sam. That's too bad."

"I'm not happy about the week's suspension."

"He could come out with us on Tuesday. We can tell Eddie-O he's just a spectator, then pay him for watching our balls."

"I don't think that's a good idea," I said.

"I guess not," she said. "What about the Open?"

"Sam's coming with me. He's my caddie."

"And if you do well enough?"

Cindy had heard me speak of my plan: qualify for a big tournament, place high enough so that I automatically qualified for the next week's event, break the gravitational pull of the club, and orbit the Tour.

"He'll stay with me till school opens," I said.

"Touring with a teenage son. Sounds like a recipe for success."

The phone rang. Land-line calls were almost always for

me. Sam's communications entered the house silently—a vibrating cell phone, an e-mail, instant messages creating a patchwork of dialog boxes on the computer screen. The phone stopped before the third ring, which meant either Sam answered or the caller had hung up.

I took a sip of wine, wondering who the caller may have been and seizing on the possibility that it was Detective Donahue calling on some pretext because, as Charlie teased, he was interested in me. I ran with this idea for a while, constructing an idyllic mental montage with music playing in the background. And then Sam stood in the porch doorway, phone in hand.

"It's Dad," he said.

In the corner of my eye, Cindy's head snapped toward me. Sam handed me the phone and walked away.

"Hello, Roger," I said, mustering as much steel as possible.

"What the hell happened at the club today, Jenny?"

"You mean with Sam?"

"Of course I mean with Sam."

"Henry Chandler accused Sam of stealing thirty dollars from his wallet. Sam denied it. I tried to find out what happened, but all I got from either of them was a lot of 'Yes, you did' and 'No, I didn't.'"

"Well, Sam gave me details," said Roger. "Significant details."

"Like what?"

"This other caddie, Kieran Boyle, is a well-known sneak."

"I heard that from Charlie."

"Sam also said it probably happened on the fourteenth hole, where the caddies wait up near the green while the golfers go down into the valley for their tee shots."

"I know the fourteenth hole, Roger."

"Sam left the bag unattended when he went into the woods to pee. He thinks this was Kieran Boyle's chance to take the money."

"He didn't tell me any of this."

"This is what I've been talking about. Sam's an adolescent. He needs to be able to communicate with a parent, and if he's not going to communicate with you, we may need to rethink our custody arrangement."

"Don't you dare, Roger. I'll fight you on that. You know I will. And we do communicate. We communicate very well. But Sam told me nothing. Ask Eddie-O. We both tried to get the story out of him."

"Sam also told me Chandler threatened him."

"At first he said he would press charges for petit larceny. I called him on that, and he backed off. Then he warned Sam about not finding him in his courtroom. I think he just wanted to scare him."

"Well, he did a damn good job of it. Pompous ass. I always knew that two-bit town judgeship would go to his head. I have a good mind to call him."

"Whatever will make you feel better," I said.

"This isn't about making me feel better. This is about protecting our son. He tells me he's been suspended, too."

"For a week," I said. "Eddie-O was very apologetic about that, but there's nothing he can do."

"Oh, really?"

I could hear that tone in Roger's voice, as if he'd just picked up the gauntlet I'd thrown at his feet.

"I don't think we should get involved with the suspension," I said. "Sam needs to learn that actions have consequences."

"What actions? He says he didn't do anything. Don't you believe him?"

"Yes, I believe him."

"Then what message are we sending him? That he can be blamed for something he didn't do?"

"It happens. It's called life."

"Not if you can prevent it."

"Maybe you can, Roger. But you're a forty-five-year-old lawyer, not a fifteen-year-old kid. Sam needs to learn how to choose his friends wisely and not give a sneak like this Boyle kid a chance to screw him."

Roger grumbled and hung up.

"Excuse me," I told Cindy, then went into the den. Sam immediately looked up from his game, a sure sign he had listened to my end of the phone call.

"Why didn't you tell me about the fourteenth hole?" I said.

"I didn't think you'd understand."

"Why? Because I'm a lady and I don't know what it's like to pee in the woods?"

"Yeah," said Sam.

I waited for more but got none.

"You could have told Eddie-O if you didn't want to tell me. This is a serious thing, Sam."

"Okay," said Sam. "Geez."

I didn't want to push any further because I didn't want to put Sam in the middle of another skirmish with Roger. Roger easily could cobble this episode into evidence that I was an incompetent, disengaged parent unworthy of custody. He'd already dragged me into one full-blown custody battle since our divorce. If I knew nothing else about my ex, I knew that he yearned to return to the sites of his former defeats.

I jammed the phone back onto its stand.

"Next time, try me," I said.

EIGHT

A WEEK SEEMED a reasonable time to wait, so the next Ladies Day, after I opened the barn and parked a number of carts on the grass patch, I headed toward the greenskeeper's cottage. Why was I doing this? I wondered. Was I truly interested in why Rick Gilbert called me the night before he died? Did I suspect in some subconscious way that those calls were connected with Kit Gilbert's doubts? Or did I just want to complicate my life?

The faded Volvo wagon was parked at the edge of the maintenance road, tight against the arborvitae. A distinctive old-car smell wafted out of the open driver's window, a mixture of rubber, moldy vinyl, and uncombusted gasoline. As I turned into the driveway, I heard the sound of grinding wheels and, at the last second, saw Quint rushing at me on a skateboard. He stopped only inches short and, in the same motion, kicked the skateboard up into his hands.

"Hi, Quint," I said.

He grunted, looked me up and down.

"Nice day."

"Too humid," he said.

He wore the same type of outfit Sam often wore: big, flat-soled sneakers, knee-length shorts with many pockets, and an oversize T-shirt splattered with urban artwork.

"I'm sorry for what happened to your dad," I said.

"You didn't do anything."

"You're right." I paused. I'd forgotten how literally he would take whatever I said. "Is your mom home?"

Quint said nothing, just pushed off and skated away. He mounted a black plastic ramp, bumped onto a metal bar, and slid along its entire length on the board's axles.

Four steps led up to a porch, and on the top step lay Duke. His front legs were splayed, paws hanging over the edge, and his head lolled sideways. His eyes were open, though, and as soon as my foot hit the bottom step he roused himself into a growl, as if associating me with the demise of his master. Holding my breath, I leaned forward and reached out with my right hand, palm down. He sniffed my wrist, whimpered once, and closed his eyes.

The porch was cluttered with rusted golf clubs, spare skateboard parts, and empty cardboard boxes. On a small table, a jelly glass stood half-filled with a blue juice. A box of crackers lay on its side, spilling a trail of crumbs.

The entry door was open. The green paint on the wooden screen door was faded to gray. There was nothing but darkness inside, though I could hear the whisk of a broom.

I knocked. The whisk continued.

"Hello," I called. "Kit?"

The whisk stopped, and a moment later a pair of eyes appeared in the dark. She approached slowly and completely materialized only inches from the screen. Housedress, slippers, dishrag twisting in her hands.

"Hi, Kit," I said.

She stared at me, her expression so disarmingly blank that I retreated into manners and introduced myself as Jenny Chase. From the pro shop.

"I know who you are," she said. "You're the one who found him. Sorry you had to get involved."

"No need to apologize."

"You're right about that. Someone had to find him sometime."

She pushed open the screen door and walked away. Taking this as an invitation, I caught the door before the spring pulled it shut and followed her.

The inside of the house was just as cluttered as the porch. Boxes were everywhere: near a bookcase with half the books tumbled out, under a desk with its drawers open, in a closet with empty plastic hangers hooked on the rod.

The kitchen, where Kit obviously had been working, reeked so powerfully of chlorine that I literally felt a rash erupt on my skin. Every cabinet and drawer hung open; every inch of counter space and tabletop was covered with glassware, pots, stacks of dishes. Kit turned on the faucet. Steam rose from the sink and into the yellowed curtains hanging across the small window that opened onto a seamless wall of arborvitae a few feet away.

"Has the club hired someone?" I said, practically shouting over the rush of water.

"No, but I'm packing up anyway."

Kit used her forearm to sweep a tangled pile of cooking utensils off the counter and into the box below.

"You didn't bring any food, did you?" she said.

I raised both arms, revealing myself as empty-handed.

"Good. I have too damn much food. Most of it Quint won't even look at. He's as particular as a cat when it comes to eating."

Kit kicked the box forward, positioning it under the next pile of utensils.

"Well, if you don't have any food, why'd you come? I don't mean to be rude, but none of you ladies ever showed any interest in visiting before."

"I could come back at a better time," I said.

"No, no. You're here now."

Kit shut the faucet. The last of the steam folded itself and disappeared into the curtains.

"Last Tuesday night," I said, "I found five calls on my caller ID log. The calls all came on Monday night between eight-thirty and ten. I wasn't home, and the caller didn't leave any message."

Kit plucked a wooden spoon off the counter and rubbed her thumb on its cracked, blackened face.

"I thought the number belonged to someone I knew. I called it back, and that detective answered. Donahue. He came to my house and looked at my caller ID, then told me the number belonged to Rick's cell phone. He was holding it when I called."

"Why did Rick call you?"

"I don't know," I said. "Neither did Donahue."

Kit held up the spoon like a looking glass. "And neither do I," she said. "But all I can say is that it makes sense."

"Because you don't believe Rick killed himself?" I said.

"Now where would you get that idea?" she said.

"Your sister."

Kit turned away, smiling. "Goddamn Jackie. She's got such an easy life, she needs to meddle in mine." She turned back to me, not smiling now. "What else did she tell you?"

"Nothing else."

"You tell her about the calls?"

"No."

"That's one good thing, anyway."

"So I thought, with your doubts, you should know about them, too," I said.

"You told me. Thanks."

"Well, why don't you believe Rick killed himself?"

"Rick wasn't the suicidal type. He just didn't have it in him. But the cops ruled it a suicide. Open and shut."

"Didn't you tell them what you thought?"

"They know what I thought." Kit flipped the spoon into the box. "You saw the pictures at the funeral. Notice how none of them were very recent? That's because there's been no family life here for a good number of years. Oh, we stayed together and we never discussed getting a divorce. But it wasn't a marriage anymore. It was a loveless partnership built on a simple deal. I took care of Quint, and Rick took care of everything else. And he did. Right down the line to the very end. You can tell all the club ladies that we're okay. We have money. We need to move, but that's a minor inconvenience because Rick left me well set up. My sister always said money solves everything. I never believed her, but now I'm thinking she might be right."

She didn't bother walking me to the door, and truth be told, I didn't much care. I stepped around Duke and down the porch steps. Quint sped across the driveway, hit the ramp sideways, and fell off the skateboard. He rolled onto his knees and waggled his wrist to make sure it wasn't broken.

As I reached the bottom of the driveway, a postal truck turned in. The driver yanked back the door, pulled up the hand brake, and swung down.

"Kit Gilbert?" he said.

"Inside." I pointed.

I watched from the edge of the arborvitae. Duke barked like crazy, but the mailman sidestepped him and knocked on the door. He handed Kit a letter and held a small computerized pad for her to sign. Kit dissolved into the darkness of the house. Duke lay back down, his barks dissipating into snarls. The mailman hopped into his truck and reversed away. Quint lay prone on the driveway, rolling his skateboard back and forth a few inches from his face.

The wailing erupted suddenly.

I ran up the porch and into the house. Kit lay in the doorway to the kitchen, beating the bare linoleum with her fists.

"No!" she wailed. "No no no no no!"

I crouched beside her and put my arm around her shoulder. She hugged me ferociously. The letter and the torn envelope lay on the floor.

"Help me, Jenny," she sobbed. "Help me."

I READ THE letter twice in the time it took me to walk back to the yard. There was some activity now: Eddie-O banging open the flaps of the tin shack, caddies playing grab-ass around the benches, women golfers trailing down from their cars. I stopped at the edge of the lilacs and read the letter one more time. I had promised Kit I would help her. Peeled her off the floor, straightened her housedress on her bony shoulders, and cuffed her with one of those firm, buck-yourself-up slaps to the face right out of a British war movie. Of course, I had no clue how to keep my promise.

I folded the letter into my pocket and unlocked the pro shop door. Inside, I changed out of my jeans and into a pleated white golf skirt about three inches shorter than my usual Ladies Day fare.

"Aren't we looking hot today?" said Cindy as we strapped our golf bags onto a cart.

"Think so?" I said.

"Oh yeah."

A CLUB PROFESSIONAL, even an assistant, did not usually belong to a social organization within the club. But given my history, I straddled both worlds. I came out of college with a B.A. in English and third-team all-American golf honors. I shunned grad school and took a job as assistant pro at Harbor Terrace Country Club. My plan was to earn my PGA card, then play my way onto the Ladies Tour. Instead, I met a young lawyer named Roger Chase, fell for him, got married, and gave up the dream. Or, to be more precise, unwittingly deferred it.

I became a club member and played with the ladies, who seemed older and stodgier than I ever saw myself becoming. Then one Tuesday the starter paired me with Cindy, Steph, and Lulu. Being a club member suddenly began to seem like fun. I also went back to grad school, got my masters and then a teaching job at a local college. Every couple of years, my dream kicked like a fetus in the womb. But Roger, bless his heart, cleverly stifled these stirrings. Sam came along. Roger made partner. We had more money than I ever dreamed possible. Then the marriage tanked.

I had three non-negotiable demands: Sam, the house, and maintaining my club membership in perpetuity. Roger capitulated or, as he liked to say, tactically retreated. There may have been no permanence in marriage, he believed, but there was even less in divorce. He hinted that no part of the settlement would be mine forever.

I taught for two more years after the divorce became final. Charlie had come in as head pro, and in May of that year, I asked for what was essentially my old job back. By August, I sent the college my letter of resignation.

But I was still a club member, and the girls were still my best friends. They were my friends before Roger, during Roger, and after Roger. I'd never admit it to them, but I needed them more than they needed me.

. . .

MY ROUND SUCKED. I sprayed tee shots into the trees, dumped routine approach shots into sand traps, and putted with the touch of a Neanderthal.

"Are you sure you're all right?" Cindy said after I gave up looking for my ball in the reeds beside the ninth green and plopped myself onto the cart.

"Fine," I said. "Remember the sine curve."

"This better be the trough," she said.

After the round, we went to the clubhouse terrace for the weekly luncheon. A waiter came to take our drink orders.

"Where's Reynaldo?" I said.

"Doesn't work here anymore," said the waiter.

"But I just saw him the other day," I said, meaning the day Rick died.

"So what?" said Cindy. "Because you see him one morning, that doesn't mean he can't leave."

Cindy never would admit it, but she was peeved at having a bad round herself.

"Why did he leave?" she asked the waiter.

"New job," the waiter said. "Somewhere."

"Maybe we didn't tip him enough," said Lulu.

Steph smiled, not sure whether her sister was joking.

Twelve collective gin and tonics later, we wended our way off the terrace. Lulu and Stephanie giggled. Cindy remained austerely reserved. I was somewhere in the middle— tipsy but not sloppy, contemplative but not quiet.

Charlie did a double take when I walked into the shop. Part of it was my skirt, which he hadn't seen earlier. The rest was my glow, courtesy of the gin and four hours in the sun. In that order.

I leaned heavily on the counter. Charlie probed my shoulder, expertly thumbing the sweet spot.

"Charlie," I said, "are we very busy right now?"

"I don't have to be," he said, and arched his eyebrows.

"I mean are we too busy for me to take an hour off?"

"No," he said, disappointed. "We aren't."

NINE

THE POLICE STATION shared a stone building with the
town court in a plaza near the train station. The small
lobby harked back to a distant, less complicated era with its
black-and-white tile floor and tall wooden desk flanked by
two illuminated balls on fluted wooden posts. The desk sergeant seemed from another era, too, with his tiny wire-
rimmed glasses and pure white hair slicked with tonic and
parted in the middle.

"Detective Donahue," I said.

"Not in."

"When will he be back?"

"Tomorrow," he said, then pointedly stared at the
length of my skirt. "But if you want to see him today, you
might catch him at the town dock."

. . .

THE HARBOR WAS a perfect square dredged out of tidal muck where the slowly meandering Poningo Creek emptied into a long, narrow inlet from the Long Island Sound. Poningo Point, a thin spit of mansions and yacht clubs, ran along the south side of the inlet; the rest of the North American continent, starting with the lower holes of Harbor Terrace Country Club, ran along the other.

I parked my car in the lot and clomped down a wooden gangway to the dock itself. It was hard not to sound like a horse. More than half the slips were empty, and a parade of boats curved between an avenue of buoys toward a haze of open water in the distance. Closer, just across the harbor, a foursome stood on the eighth tee and impatiently switched their golf clubs in the sun. It always struck me, during my rare visits to this side of the inlet, how small and silly the golf course looked from this angle. I spotted Donahue quickly. The slips were in the shape of a large E, and his was the farthest out along what would be the top horizontal bar. He was sitting on the edge of the slip, his feet dangling in the water, while he rubbed a piece of brass with a cheesecloth. When he spotted me coming, he put everything aside and stood up.

"Well, well," he said, wiping his hands on his shorts, "to what do I owe this honor?"

"Rick Gilbert," I said.

A frown crossed his face—maybe he hoped this was a purely social visit, I thought—but he recovered quickly and shook my hand. He wore a faded green tank top, and his biceps and shoulders continued the same well-muscled theme of his forearms. He stepped over the gunwale onto his boat and held out his hand.

"We're not sailing away," he said. "It's the only place we can sit."

I took his hand and stepped in. The name *Maggie May* was lettered in green cursive on the stern. The sailboat had two masts, and I knew enough to realize that the number of masts and the cut of the sails held fine distinctions.

"What kind of boat is this?" I said.

"A ketch," he said, "with some variations. Are you familiar with the normal configuration?"

I shook my head.

"Well, then I won't get into the details. They'd bore the heck out of you."

We sat on cushioned benches.

"Are you a Rod Stewart fan?" I said. "The name."

Rather than answer, Donahue turned away.

"Do you see anyone out there?" he said.

"Where?" I cupped a hand over my eyes.

"The harbor. Swimming."

Almost immediately, a dot broke the surface near the tumble of boulders at the base of the cliff below the eighth tee.

"Danny!" yelled Donahue. "That's too far."

The dot resolved into the head of a boy. He waved and shot forward, ripping the water with powerful strokes. Donahue settled back slowly and returned his attention to me.

"My son," he said. "Loves the water. He can swim all day. A harbor seal was here last week. He wants to catch it and ride it."

"Cute," I said.

"You were saying?"

"The name of the boat. Is it from the Rod Stewart song?"

"Maggie's my late wife. May is the month we met." He slapped his knees. "I'm sorry. I'm being a terrible host. Do you want something to drink?"

"I'm fine," I said, though in fact I wasn't. Donahue had been floating on the periphery of my consciousness for the last week, lending a not unpleasant buoyancy to my mood. I suddenly felt dragged down, and I wasn't sure why. I don't think it was Danny; after all, I already knew he had a teenage son. More likely it was how he had allowed me to walk right into the memory of his dead wife.

"I never knew you were a sailor," I added lamely, and hoped some of my glow remained.

"You never knew I existed till last Tuesday." He gave another quick glance toward Danny, then took a deep breath and spread his arms along the gunwale behind him. "The boat's a hobby. It was a wreck when I bought it, and two years of solid work later it's almost seaworthy. But I take the long view. It's like a minivacation to spend my days off here. I work. Danny helps me until he gets bored and jumps into the water. When I retire, he and I will take a long cruise. He wants to go around the world. I tell him the Horn of Florida might be more like it."

He lifted a cushion and plunged his hand into a cooler. "Second chance?"

"No thanks."

He popped the top of a seltzer can and took a long swig.

His eyes slipped off mine and settled on a generous patch of sun-reddened thigh. I uncrossed my legs and leaned forward, my elbows on my knees.

"So, Rick Gilbert," he said. "Did you find out why he called you last Monday night?"

"No," I said, then added after a beat, "what if I did? Would it make any difference?"

"With what?"

"Your conclusion."

"I doubt it," he said. "Why?"

I unfolded the letter from my purse and handed it to him.

"I went to Kit's house this morning to ask if she knew about those calls. The timing couldn't have been worse. She was packing up her house and telling me that as soon as her money came through, she was moving. This arrived as I left the house, registered mail."

Donahue quickly read the first page, then let out a long whistle.

"Disclaiming on a two-million-dollar insurance policy," he said. "She must feel terrible."

"She's hysterical," I said. "Literally collapsed onto the floor. Who wouldn't? Her husband's dead, she's getting thrown out of her house, she has a son who needs constant attention. He's autistic, you know."

"I know," said Donahue. He rubbed the back of his neck.

"I thought you handled him beautifully that morning when he jumped you," I said. "Another person would have retaliated. But you knew exactly what to do."

"One of my many talents," he said. "Anyway, suicide

exclusions are common. Is there any way the insurance company will reconsider?"

"Read the second page."

Donahue slipped the first page under the second. I could see the upside-down print and knew what it said by heart.

IN THE EVENT LOCAL AUTHORITIES UNCOVER EVIDENCE THAT THE INSURED DID NOT COM-MIT SUICIDE, WE WILL INITIATE OUR OWN IN-VESTIGATION AND RECONSIDER YOUR CLAIM.

"You are the local authorities," I said.

"I understand that, Jenny. But why are you here and not her?"

"She doesn't know I'm here. She asked me to help, and I told her I would try, and the first thing that came to mind was talking to you."

"The case is closed," he said.

"Can it be reopened?"

"Jenny, Rick Gilbert killed himself. Why did he do it? I don't know. Do I feel bad for his family? Damn right I do. But I can't reopen a case because I feel bad for the family."

"Kit doesn't believe Rick killed himself," I said.

"She doesn't? I questioned her for a good half hour, and she said nothing to me. Why does she think so now? Because of this letter?"

"The letter hadn't arrived yet," I said. "I told her about the calls. She said they 'made sense.' "

"What sense?"

"She didn't elaborate. But she went off, telling me they had a loveless marriage. She took care of Quint, he took care of everything else. Exact words. Which is why she doesn't believe Rick killed himself. She says he wouldn't have left her like that."

"He left her a two-million-dollar insurance policy, didn't he?"

"One that she can't collect on."

"This is going in circles, Jenny."

"Okay," I said. "What would you need to reopen the case?"

He scratched the back of his neck. "I would need substantial evidence pointing to an alternate theory."

"Like what, for instance?"

"A death threat."

"What about those phone calls?"

"They aren't evidence of anything."

"What if he was trying to tell me something?"

"Like what? You said you hardly spoke to him."

"Maybe he was trying to contact Roger."

"But Roger's been out of your house for four years." He took another big swig of seltzer. "Look, what happened is that Rick killed himself. Ninety percent of the time the obvious, banal explanation is what actually did happen."

"What about the other ten percent?"

"Mysteries don't happen in a town like ours."

"Suppose I find something?"

"You?" He swallowed a laugh.

"What's so funny?"

"Nothing." He bit the inside of his mouth. He wasn't

quite smirking, but his facial muscles could have arranged themselves into a big grin if he let go. "Are you going to investigate Rick Gilbert's death?"

"Kit asked for my help. Who else is going to do it?"

"Someone in her situation should hire a private investigator."

"She doesn't have the money for that."

Donahue took a deep breath. I'd convinced him of something, though I didn't think it was my competence.

"Bring me whatever you find," he said. "I can't promise you I'll reopen the case, but I promise you I'll look into any legitimate lead."

"Thanks, Detective."

"It's George," he said.

I stood up. The ketch yawed, and I almost lost my balance before Donahue caught me.

"Thanks," I said, and smoothed my skirt over my hips. "George."

THE GARFIELD READING Room was located at the top of a T intersection formed by Poningo and Elm. It had large front display windows, a recessed entryway, and a cornerstone with a year from early in the last century chiseled in Roman numerals.

A bell tinkled quaintly as I opened the front door. Eric Garfield blocked the main aisle, deep in conversation with an obviously moneyed older woman.

"The author is pseudonymous," he said, rubbing his hands together. "But I suspect he or she either lives or lived in Poningo. The setting definitely is our little town."

"I don't like mysteries," said the woman.

"Ah, but that's exactly the point," said Eric. "This is a mystery for people who don't like mysteries."

I detoured down the classics aisle, picking up a faint aroma of tea as I circled into self-help. Eric's original conception of the Reading Room had only three sections: classics, highbrow, and middlebrow. He didn't stock best sellers, he didn't stock trashy novels, he didn't stock any nonfiction (no matter how sophisticated the subject or erudite the author), and he didn't stock the kinds of mystery novels he was trying to sell to this woman at that very moment. It was a lousy business plan. The store teetered on the brink of bankruptcy on several occasions, and each time Eric allowed Cindy to create another section. The result was financial security and a store that looked like any other bookstore, except for Eric, who trolled the aisles and handsold his personal favorites to his regular customers. I had been a regular myself once, taking Eric's recommendations of little-known books to illuminate the dark corners of the courses I taught. Like the Burgess novel Cindy had noticed in my bookcase the other night.

The suicide subsection of self-help was on a bottom shelf. I rolled a stepstool into position and hunkered down. I could hear Eric droning on about the pseudonymous author, I could hear the distinctive tap-tapping of Cindy's silver tea ball against the rim of her mug. There were a surprising number of books about suicide, both assisted and unassisted. I didn't care about medical ethics. I needed to know the basics: who committed suicide and why.

"Did you quit?"

I looked up. Cindy loomed over me. She still wore her golf togs, but her glow was gone.

"Took an hour off." I stood up and checked my watch. "I have fifteen minutes left."

"Want some? Water's still hot." She took a slurping sip that was two parts air and one part tea. "That was some lunch. Need to flush the gin out of me. Did I say anything stupid?"

"No more than usual."

"Thanks. Forget the tea." She set her mug onto an empty patch of shelf. "What the hell are you doing in self-help?"

"I need a primer on suicide."

"Why?"

"What do you mean, why? Do you grill all your customers?"

"Jenny, you've probably bought a hundred books from us, but you've never once walked into our self-help section."

"There is a first time for everything."

Cindy frowned. "I'm getting the feeling today's round wasn't part of the sine curve. Something was bothering you."

I told her about the phone calls from Rick, my visit with Kit Gilbert that morning, the letter from the insurance company, and my promise to help.

"Is this about helping Kit or about the investigating detective being a hunk?" said Cindy.

"How did you know? You were at Westchester with me that day."

"Word spread through the ladies like a hormonal secretion."

"I confess there was an element of that at first," I said. "But no more."

"Married with children?"

"You're half-right," I said. "He has a teenage son and a dead wife he still pines over."

"He admitted that?"

"Not specifically, but he named his boat after her."

"A boat?" Cindy slurped another sip of tea. "Interesting."

"Anyway," I said, "if I learn about the patterns and people who commit suicide, I'll know whether Rick Gilbert's suicide fits any of those patterns. If it does, so be it. If it doesn't, maybe the police will reopen the investigation and maybe Kit can collect her insurance money."

"You're really going to investigate this?" Cindy laughed.

"Don't laugh," I said. I meant it. "You're the second person to laugh at this."

"Who was the first?"

"George."

"George is it now?" said Cindy.

"He insisted," I said.

"I see." Cindy reached down to the lower shelf but straightened right back up again. "I'm not sure I want to be a party to you blowing your shot at the Open."

"You won't because I won't."

Cindy stared at me hard. I knew exactly what she was thinking. For her, I was the perfect embodiment of the symbol of Pisces: two fish swimming in opposite directions. No matter what I planned or where I headed, something could turn me around. But then she softened, realizing, I suppose, that denying me a book wouldn't stop me from swimming upstream.

"This is your book." Cindy grabbed a book from the shelf and hid it behind her back. "But I'm not selling it to you."

"Why not?"

"Because buying it is a waste of your money. All you need to know is the title."

"If I can see it."

Cindy relented and handed me the book. The title was *The Three D's of Suicide: Debt, Disease, Despair.*

"I get it," I said. "These are the three main reasons a person commits suicide. Eliminate them from Rick Gilbert's life and maybe I can convince George to reopen the case."

"But be careful," said Cindy. "If you rule out the three D's, you don't just prove that Rick didn't kill himself. You prove that someone else did."

TEN

WHEN I GOT back to the cottage, I found a mud-spattered electric cart parked at the bottom of the porch steps. Quint sat in the driver's seat, groaning imitation engine noises and twisting the steering wheel from side to side. Duke sat next to him, unfazed by the racket, his front paws propped on the dash.

The cottage door opened, and a man wearing dark green overalls and a yellow shirt stepped onto the porch. Kit came out behind the man, whom I recognized as Guy Amodeo, Rick's longtime assistant greenskeeper. They spoke briefly, though I couldn't hear what they said over Quint's engine sounds. Guy shoved a large contractor's tape measure into his pocket. He reached out his right hand, and reluctantly, it seemed to me, Kit offered hers in return.

Guy came down the steps and stood beside Quint. The boy paid him no mind. He kicked his imaginary engine into a higher, louder gear and leaned into a sharp make-believe turn. One flying elbow butted Guy in the chest.

"Quint," Kit called from the porch. She repeated his name several more times, while Guy stood by helplessly. Finally, Kit came down the steps and wrapped her arms around her son.

"Quint," she said. "Quint. Why don't you show Mr. Amodeo one of your skateboard tricks."

Quint didn't cut his engine immediately. He wound down into a lower gear and slammed on the imaginary brakes. Then he extricated himself from his mother's arms, ducked out of the cart, and ran to his skateboard. He hit the board full force, flew up the ramp, and skidded the length of the metal grinding bar.

Guy climbed into the cart and elbowed Duke off the other side. The dog hit the pavement with a grunt and shook himself off. Guy reversed the cart past me without any acknowledgment. He was a distant image in my mind, perpetually driving some sort of maintenance vehicle out on the fringes of the golf course. Up close, he seemed more of a caricature than a person, with a big head of curly dark hair and a thick matching mustache. I could see now that he colored both.

Kit obviously was trying not to cry as I reached the porch. Her eyes were moist and her mouth tight. A nerve in her neck twitched.

"Ma, watch!" yelled Quint.

The sound of his wheels changed as he went from pavement to ramp and back to pavement again.

"He was here to measure my house," Kit told me. "He applied for Rick's job. He thinks he's getting it."

"Oh, Kit," I said.

"He said I could stay if I needed to. He doesn't have much furniture. He said we could live like brother and sister." A tear hurried down her cheek. She wiped it away and swallowed hard.

I handed her the letter.

"That's it?" she said. "You're done?"

"No," I said. "Just beginning. I talked to Detective Donahue."

"He'll reopen the case?" said Kit.

"Not yet. And not without us convincing him at the very least that Rick had no reason to kill himself. I need two things, your financial records and Rick's medical records."

"Why those?"

"Debt and disease are two of the leading reasons people commit suicide," I said. I didn't explain the source of my sudden expertise.

"We aren't in debt, and he wasn't sick," said Kit.

"You may be right, but we need to prove that to Detective Donahue."

"I don't know where Rick kept any medical records. He was never sick, except for one winter when his elbow swelled up from an infection. He went for yearly checkups to a doctor in town."

"Which doctor?"

"Preston."

What a stroke of luck. Of all the doctors in town, Rick used the right one.

"What about finances?" I said.

"Come with me," said Kit.

We went into the cottage and up the stairs to a hall closet. Kit dragged out a plastic milk crate from a closet. The crate was stuffed with file folders, manila envelopes, bank statements, and canceled checks.

"Rick kept everything here," she said. "He did all the banking, paid the bills, wrote every check except for when he had that arm infection and couldn't hold a pen. I wrote the checks for a couple of months. He stood over me and told me what to do."

From down below came the click-clack, click-clack, of Quint practicing kick flips. I gripped the crate firmly with both hands and lifted it to my waist. It weighed a ton. As I turned toward the door, a yellow credit card slip fluttered out. Kit scraped it off the floor.

"My birthday dinner two years ago." She smiled distantly. "I told him we shouldn't spend this much, but he insisted."

She thumbed open a folder and pushed the slip inside.

I followed her down the stairs, the bottom edge of the crate cutting sharply into the flesh above my knees with each step. Kit peered through the front door. The click-clacking had stopped, and Quint sat Indian style on the driveway with his back against the arborvitae. His skateboard lay upside down across his lap, and he spun each of the wheels in turn.

"Rick always told me I would be all right if anything ever happened to him," said Kit. "He meant the insurance policy. He had to. Why would he pay all that money for a policy and then kill himself?"

"We'll take it one step at a time," I said. "Whatever we find we'll bring to Detective Donahue. He strikes me as a reasonable guy."

"Thank you, Jenny," she said, her face brightening for a moment.

Wanting to avoid false hope, I said nothing else, just squeezed through the door. Duke was gone. I could hear him barking somewhere behind the cottage, no doubt at a golfer whose ball had strayed too close to Duke's turf.

Quint rolled up to me in the driveway.

"That's Daddy's stuff," he said.

"I know, Quint. Your mom gave it to me."

"Why?"

"I'm helping Mom with something," I said.

"Help Mom," said Quint. He did a kick flip. "Help Daddy." He did another kick flip. "Help help help help help."

He rolled behind me until I reached the edge of the parking lot. Then he let me go.

LATE AFTERNOON, AND the shop was unusually quiet. The heat had driven most of the golfers off the course and into the pool. Charlie was at his workbench in the bag room, replacing the grips on a set of clubs. I stood behind the counter, wading through all the checks Rick Gilbert had written in the last eighteen months.

Lulu came in shortly after four with a red cardboard file.

"From Steph," she said. "She wants it back fast. The

doctor doesn't know. If he finds out . . ." She slashed a finger across her throat.

"Tell her not to worry," I said.

Lulu lifted one of the checks, then walked her finger across the top of the crate.

"Why all the Rick Gilbert stuff?" she said.

"Kit has an insurance problem," I said. I started to explain, but Lulu already knew. Cindy had told her.

"Just be careful," she said.

"I will," I said. "And thank Cindy for her concern."

An hour passed, along with another eighteen months of checks. The checks repeated themselves in monthly cycles, telling me nothing other than that Rick paid his bills on time. The life insurance checks appeared about three years earlier. The premium was $253 per month.

I stuffed the checks back into their envelopes and opened the medical file. After five minutes, I closed that and put my head down on the counter. The glass felt cool, then warmed up.

What the hell had I gotten myself into? I wondered. My major talent was golf and my minor was analyzing literature, not medicine or forensic accounting. How could I expect to help Kit Gilbert? Why would I even try?

"Ahem."

I jumped up, startled. Charlie stood across the counter, wiping his hands on a greasy towel. He reeked of the gasoline he injected into old club grips to break the adhesive bonds.

"Damn, Charlie, you scared me," I said, pressing a hand to my palpitating heart.

He said nothing, just fixed a stare at the stuff on the counter.

"Rick's financial and medical records," I said.

"Okay," Charlie said slowly, begging the question, which was, What the hell are you doing with them?

"I'm trying to help Kit Gilbert collect on a two-million-dollar insurance policy. The company disclaimed under a suicide clause."

"You're investigating Rick's death?" He had the good sense not to comment on the timing of my endeavor, but the thought hung in the air between us as obvious as cigar smoke.

"Not really," I said. "More like I'm trying to convince the insurance company to reconsider the claim, which entails convincing the police to reopen the case. Detective Donahue told me he'd look at whatever I found."

Charlie stepped to the counter. "So this is your investigation? A crate of papers and a medical file?"

"Cindy's idea," I said.

"Cindy." Charlie raised his eyes to the ceiling "heaven help us" style.

"It's from a book. *The Three D's of Suicide*. These are two of them." I patted each. "Debt and disease."

"What's the third? Drug dependency? No, that would be four D's."

"You mock me, Charlie."

"Not at all." He poked through the crate, then riffled the medical file. "You're feeling overwhelmed, right?"

"How did you know?"

Charlie said nothing, just gave a little shake to his head

that made me wonder how long he'd been watching me and, beyond that, how totally at sea I must have appeared to him. No matter how disorganized Charlie looked on the surface, he could read people like nobody's business.

He fished in his pocket for his keys.

"Put the medical file in my car. I'll have it back to you tomorrow morning."

"What are you going to do?"

"Look to see if Rick had a terminal disease. That's what you're hoping not to find, right?"

"Yes, but—"

"You don't expect me to analyze his finances when I don't even understand my own, do you?"

"No."

"Well, then, why the look?"

"What do you know about medicine?" I said.

"What do I know about medicine?" said Charlie. "I was pre-med at Maryland before the siren song of a golf career called."

THE PORCH AT night: Music played softly on the portable stereo. Sweat beaded on two tall glasses of iced tea. Fireflies climbed in the darkened backyard. The ceiling fan turned slowly so as not to disturb the piles of paper Cindy arranged on the table. Cindy had her silver hair pulled back and gathered with a rubber band. The sleeves of her pink button-down Oxford were rolled to her elbows.

"That about wraps it up." She closed a file folder over a pile of credit card vouchers and began returning all of the papers to the crate. "The Gilbert family is no different from most everyone else. They carry credit card debt they couldn't pay off if the loans were called all at once. But the loans aren't called, and the national economy moves forward like the big Ponzi scheme that it is."

"I didn't know you were such an economic theorist," I said.

"I'm not. One of my new book orders arrived today. *The Coming Crash: How Personal Debt Will Destroy the U.S. Economy*."

"Do all your orders have colons in the title?"

"Lately, yes. They are so dramatic. Like a musical flourish. Ta-da." Cindy laughed. "Eric didn't mind the suicide book so much. He hates this one."

"For once, I agree. Who's going to buy that book in this town?"

"You would be surprised," said Cindy. "People like a good scare. They like it even better if there is a controlled element of personal danger. Reading *The Coming Crash* is like riding the Dragon Coaster. They can get the willies, then close the book and put it back on the shelf where they think it can't hurt them."

Cindy sat back and drew her iced tea onto her lap. "That rules out debt," she said. "Now what?"

"Steph sent me Rick's medical file," I said. "Rick was a regular patient there. Charlie's looking at the file."

"Charlie!" Cindy practically sprayed me with iced tea.

"Yeah, Charlie. He was pre-med at Maryland. He knows what to look for."

"Okay, Jen. Don't get so defensive."

We sipped awhile in silence. A moth began ticking

against the screen. I shut off the pharmacy lamp I'd dragged out for extra light. The front door opened and slammed shut, causing several candles on the table to gutter and then steady.

"I'm home," called Sam.

"Hi, hon," I called back. "Cindy's here. We're on the porch. Come say hi."

Sam came only as far as the doorway. I conducted a quick visual inspection, then kissed his forehead. No tell-tale odor.

"I'm going to bed," he said. "Tired."

His footsteps faded on the stairs. Cindy sighed.

"Depending on what Charlie finds," she said, "that leaves only despair. How are you going to handle that?"

"I don't know," I said. "Honestly, the more I think about it, I wish we'd found something tonight. Or I wish Charlie tells me something tomorrow. Makes things easier for me, but of course hard for Kit."

"You can't live her life for her. You have the Open coming up, plus your own issues here." Cindy meant Sam. "How has he been with the suspension?"

"Rather good, actually," I said. "He's hardly been in front of the TV. He's already read one of his two summer reading list books. He took out the garbage without my asking tonight. And he's even offered to shag balls for me after work."

"Something's up," said Cindy.

"I've thought that, too."

ELEVEN

NEXT MORNING, THERE were three police cars parked in front of the clubhouse. A curtain hung out of an open window, and a cop stood in the flower bed beneath it as if on guard duty. A stocky man with dark hair stood with the locker-room attendant under the porte cochere. The man jotted notes in a tiny notebook, the same type of notebook Donahue used. Another detective, I concluded. Funny how you start to notice these details when you know what to look for.

Down on the pro shop patio, Charlie drank coffee and chewed a buttered roll.

"Somebody broke into the locker room last night and roughed up the vending machines," he said.

"I'm beginning to feel that we've moved to the outskirts of civilization here," I said.

"A bad stretch, that's for sure."

Charlie pulled a second container of coffee from a paper bag and set it in front of me.

"I combed through Rick's medical file last night," he said.

"And?"

"Rick had nothing terribly wrong. Mild hypertension that he controlled with medication. Borderline high cholesterol that the doctor wasn't concerned about because he had good HDL numbers. He went for annual physicals every March. The last one showed him perfectly fit for a man his age. He had a serious strep infection in his arm about ten years ago. Spent two weeks in the hospital and had four debriding surgeries. Came out fine. That was it. Nothing malign lurking in the shadows."

Up the hill, the detective joined the cop in the flower bed. They crouched to inspect the ground.

"Thanks," I told Charlie.

After we pulled out some carts and opened the shop, I lugged the milk crate to the cottage. Duke charged, sniffed me quickly, then turned away. My novelty had worn off.

Kit sat on the porch. The clutter from a few days ago was completely gone. A cardboard box labeled "TOYS" stood in a corner, its flaps sealed with brown packing tape.

I set the crate on the table.

"Quiet here," I said.

"Quint's at a friend's house," she said. "A long time ago, we were part of a play group with a few other autistic boys. It fell apart as the boys got older because their different levels of functioning made the matchups difficult. But for a while it was my only break."

"Were those the boys I saw at the cemetery?" I said.

"Some of them." Kit stared wistfully into the middle distance, then shook herself back. "He rarely gets invited anywhere now. When he does, it feels like . . . I hate to say this . . . it feels like a vacation."

"I'll leave you and—"

"No." She kicked a chair out from the table. "Sit. This is nice. Just me and another adult."

I sat.

"Tell me," she said. "What did you find? Am I bankrupt?"

"No, you're not bankrupt."

"Oh." She sounded disappointed.

"That's a good thing, Kit. It means Rick didn't kill himself because he was horribly in debt."

"But Rick didn't kill himself at all."

"I know. But we're trying to prove that by ruling out the obvious reasons."

Slowly, Kit swept invisible crumbs off the table.

"I also had someone look at Rick's medical records." I didn't want to say that someone was Charlie; this investigation seemed amateurish enough already. "He didn't have a dread disease."

"Then that's good, too. Right?"

"Yes, but it leaves open the toughest question." I tapped a finger against my temple. "What was going on in Rick's head last week?"

Kit chuckled mirthlessly. "If you only knew how tough a question," she said. "Rick rarely said anything about anything. You think we ever sat down like this and talked?

Never. Quint always was around. And at night, when Quint finally fell asleep, we were both too tired.

"But fatigue was only an excuse. Rick just kept things to himself. He knew I had my hands full dealing with Quint, so he just took care of things without bothering me and then without bothering to tell me. Like our finances. One Christmas, Rick wanted to buy this big plastic car with an electric motor for Quint. It cost something like three hundred dollars, which was a huge amount for us to spend on a single gift. I asked Rick how we could afford it, and he said his bonus. What bonus? I asked. It turned out that he was getting a bonus from the club each year and not telling me.

"And I guess," she said, "keeping things to himself became a habit he just couldn't break. I would find something out, like long after the fact, and get mad. I would remind him that I was his wife, that I wanted to help him with his problems because that was what a wife did. Sometimes we would argue, sometimes he would promise to share his problems with me. But it almost never happened. Like that lawsuit. I had no idea Rick was being sued."

"What lawsuit?" I said. Her tone sounded as if she expected me to know.

"The people on Soundview. The chemicals."

Soundview was a narrow, tree-shrouded road of relatively modest homes that bisected the golf course and dwindled into a patch of sand near the ninth green without ever reaching the harbor.

I shook my head.

"A few years ago, an exotic weed started taking over the

fairway grass. The greens committee basically ordered Rick to get rid of the weed or lose his job. Rick tried everything. He was on the Internet every day researching all kinds of chemicals. Finally, he came up with a mix of chemical herbicides and organic fertilizers. The mix killed the weed, and everyone was happy."

"Was this what the greens chairman mentioned at the funeral?" I said.

"Yes."

Other than that, I remembered nothing about this problem, which surprised me. Bothered me, too. I prided myself on paying attention to my surroundings and on maintaining an accurate, coherent chronology of my personal past.

"How long ago was that?" I said.

"Five years," said Kit. "No. Four. Definitely four. It was toward the end of that summer. We had Quint's twelfth birthday party, and I was mad at Rick for spending too much time on the phone about the problem."

The end of summer four years ago. That explained why I had no memory. Roger served me with papers on August 1, and for the rest of the year the divorce proceedings obscured my view of everything around me.

"The next year," Kit continued, "the club got sued. This little girl living on Soundview came down with cancer, and her parents believed she got it from the chemicals Rick used to kill that weed. What I didn't know, and what Rick didn't tell me till long after, was that the club basically screwed him. They denied giving Rick the authority to use those chemicals, even though they threatened to fire him if he couldn't kill that weed. So Rick was hung out to dry. We could have lost everything, but one of the members volunteered to represent Rick for free and got him out of the case."

"That was fortunate," I said.

Kit smiled quickly.

"Anyway, you asked about what was in Rick's head last week, and all I can say is that about three, maybe four weeks ago, someone stuck a letter for Rick in our mailbox. I put the letter on the radiator cover with the rest of the mail. Rick took care of the mail the way he took care of the bills, meaning he opened all the mail unless it was a personal letter addressed only to me. He was very quick. Most of the mail he ripped up without ever opening it. Especially the credit card applications. He hated them.

"I watched him go through the mail that day. It was cool and rainy. He was wearing a windbreaker. When he got to that letter, he looked at it and folded it into his windbreaker pocket.

"I asked him about that letter sometime later. He said it was nothing. I said it didn't seem like nothing since someone took the trouble of putting it directly into our mailbox. Was it from someone at the club, or one of the committees? I asked. And he looked at me very seriously and said, 'I don't know.'

"About a week later, this lawyer named Terry Silverman called. She specializes in education law, and we've hired her to make sure Quint gets all the school services he's entitled to. Did you know that our school district has one of the best programs for autistic children in the county? Kids come here from all the surrounding towns. Anyway, she told me she'd been trying to call Rick's cell phone but couldn't reach him. She said to tell him she had those names for him.

"I gave Rick the message, and we ended up in one of our usual arguments. I was very hard on him. I told him what was the point of shielding me from his problems when the worst thing that could possibly happen already did." Kit paused. "I meant Quint."

We sat in silence for a long moment. Even Duke noticed. He whimpered and dropped a paw over the edge of the porch. Kit went inside. A minute later, she came back out with a green-and-yellow windbreaker draped over her arm. She punched her hand into one pocket and then the other. Both times she came up empty.

"It was worth a try," she said.

"Maybe he ripped it up."

"Maybe."

"What was the connection between the letter and the call from the lawyer?"

"Nothing," said Kit, "except for what I feel here."

She touched her heart.

TWELVE

TERRY SILVERMAN'S LAW office was a second-floor walk-up above a picture-framing shop half a block off Poningo on Elm. The door was open, and a blond woman with hard features sat at a reception desk. Several pages of typescript were spread on the desk, and I immediately saw the woman was proofreading. Politely, I waited for her to look up.

"Is Ms. Silverman in?"

"I am Ms. Silverman," she said. She sounded annoyed at being taken for someone else.

I introduced myself and explained that I was helping Kit Gilbert with an insurance problem. She gathered her pages together and led me into her own office.

"What kind of insurance problem?" she said. She may have been more comfortable behind her own desk, but she didn't look any happier.

"You know what happened," I said. She nodded. "Rick

Gilbert had a two-million-dollar life insurance policy, but the company disclaimed under a suicide clause."

"Let me guess," said Terry Silverman. "The company said it would reconsider the claim only if the police reopened the investigation."

"Right," I said. "And one of the things I'm helping Kit track down is a letter someone stuck in their mailbox about three weeks ago. Kit thinks Rick called you about the letter."

"Me?" said Terry Silverman. "Called me? What did this letter say?"

"She doesn't know. She never actually read it."

"She never read it, but she knows Rick called me about it."

"It's what she thinks," I said. "And you did speak to her on the phone. You said you had some names for Rick but you couldn't reach him on his cell phone."

Terry Silverman took a deep breath. She lifted those same pages, tapped their edges together, and laid them back down on the desk.

"I've known the Gilberts ever since they retained me to obtain pre-school special ed services for Quint. I consider the Gilbert family to be friends, not just clients. I'm sorry about what happened to Rick. I'm sorry for him, I'm sorry for Quint, and I'm especially sorry for Kit because she'll bear the brunt of all this. But I don't know about any letter."

"Then why did you call Rick's house? Why did you tell Kit you had some names for Rick?"

"Rick called me," she said. "It was about three weeks ago. He said he had a problem. He didn't want to discuss the particulars with me. He said they were 'embarrassing.'

All he said was that it wasn't quite a legal problem, but it could turn into one. I took that to mean he needed to get someone off his back."

"Do you mean like threaten someone who was threatening him?"

She jumped right over that.

"I told him I would get back to him with some names. I did. I called his cell phone, and when he didn't call me back I called the house and spoke to Kit. Another day passed. Rick still didn't call back. I thought maybe the problem resolved itself and Rick didn't need the names anymore. But on the off chance that it didn't, I left the names on his cell phone."

"So theoretically," I said, "Rick could have gotten those names and he could have called one of them."

"I suppose so," said Terry Silverman.

"Can you tell me who they are?"

Terry Silverman took another one of her deep breaths. I'd been with her less than five minutes but could see they were her way of controlling conversations.

"Look, miss," she said, "this is a small legal community, and I have a very narrow practice that depends on referrals from other lawyers. I'm not going to start blabbing names so you can bother these other lawyers like you're bothering me."

OUT ON THE street, the passenger window rolled down on an idling gray sedan and a voice called my name. I leaned down to look.

"Why, George," I said. "Hello."

"I went to the club to see you," said Donahue. "Your boss told me you were playing detective."

I made a mental note to yell at Charlie.

"You have a moment to talk?"

"Sure," I said.

"Hop in."

I did. He shoved off from the curb and tooled down Elm. A set of plastic rosary beads dangled from the rearview mirror. A tiny notebook was wedged between us into the seam of the seat.

"I came by," he said, "because I wanted to see how your investigation was going."

"Fine," I said. "Clues upon clues. Why? Did you find something?"

"Quite the opposite. I'm planning to archive the file."

"What does that mean?" I said. "Move it from one file cabinet to another?"

"No," said Donahue. "If we kept every file we ever created, we'd run out of room pretty damn quick. There's a facility up county that stores archived files for all the local departments. The files get scanned and stored in a central computer bank, and I can bring any file up on my desktop whenever I need it. That's the good news. The bad news is that the facility is months behind in scanning and files sometimes get lost."

I felt my insides shift, as though I slipped on ice and caught myself before I fell. If George archived that file, the case never would be reopened.

"You can't do that, George," I said.

"I'm sorry. We have our rules. And I'm not just doing this. I went back over every word in the file to see if there was anything I missed, anything I could possibly use as a reason to reopen the investigation. I found nothing."

"I have an idea," I said. "Give the file to me if you need to get it out of your office so badly."

"I can't do that, either, Jen."

"What will it take for you to hold on to that file a little longer?" I said. I didn't mean it like that, and George, ever the perfect gentleman, didn't take it that way.

"I need you to find something that gives me a legitimate reason not to archive the file."

We reached the end of Elm. Donahue turned left, heading in the general direction of the club. I wished I had something concrete to tell him. All I had were Kit's feelings and my own vague suspicions after speaking to Terry Silverman; at the moment, neither was enough.

"I've ruled out Rick being in debt or having a terminal disease," I said.

Donahue took his eyes off the road. "How'd you do that?"

"Looked through his financial and medical records."

"Not bad," he said. "That removes two common reasons for suicide from the equation."

"You read the book?" I said.

"What book?"

"Never mind." I told him about the letter.

"But the wife never saw it," he said when I finished. "And she doesn't know for sure whether Rick called Terry

Silverman about the letter or whether Terry Silverman's call to the house was about the letter. And Terry Silverman refused to discuss any of this with you."

"Right, right, and right," I said.

"Did she refuse because of the attorney-client privilege?"

"She didn't say that," I said. "I just don't think she liked me."

"Didn't like you?" Donahue smiled playfully. "I can't believe that."

"It happens. But it's rare. And the people who don't take an immediate shine to me usually have serious psychological problems and often find themselves institutionalized."

"Is she still in her office?" he said.

"Was when I left."

He turned back toward Elm. He didn't say a word until he parked in front of the framing shop, and then he only said, "Wait here."

I sat, listening to the clicks of the sedan's engine as it cooled. In the framing shop's window hung a huge canvas of an English cottage. Wildflowers engulfed a white picket fence. Willows reflected on the surface of a narrow river. In the middle distance, a stone bridge arched across the river, and beyond a white steeple rose above the horizon. *My life,* I thought. *My tidy little organized life before Rick Gilbert died. I wanted to crawl back into it.*

I didn't see Donahue until the car shook and he climbed behind the wheel.

"Well, it wasn't just you," he said. "I didn't get anywhere with her, either."

"Attorney-client privilege?"

"No. Female obstinacy," he said. "Sorry. I didn't mean that the way it sounded."

"Can't you force her to tell you?" I said. "I'm just a woman off the street. You're a detective."

"Sure I could force her. I could bring her down to the station and grill her. Or I could ask the town attorney to issue a subpoena. But to do either of those things I need an active investigation and a pretty good idea of what I'm looking for. Right now, I don't have either."

"What if I find the letter?"

"That," he said, "would change everything."

I got out of the car and leaned down to the window.

"And here I thought she would jump into your arms. Figuratively."

"Sometimes people don't like me, either," he said.

THIRTEEN

BACK AT THE club, I went directly to the greenskeeper's cottage. The Volvo was gone from the driveway, and Quint's skateboard hung by its wheels on the porch railing. I scribbled a note, folded it twice, and wedged it between the screen door and the jamb. The note stressed the importance of Kit finding the letter.

In the pro shop, Charlie slumped forlornly behind the counter. At the sight of me, he glanced upward in a combination of thanksgiving and exasperation.

"Playing?" I said. "You told Donahue I was playing detective?"

"Now, Jen, I didn't mean that literally, like you were having fun."

"You better not. Because this definitely is not fun." I noticed a pile of green on the counter, like a picked-apart salad. "What's this?"

"The morning's sales." He held up a legal pad. "I wrote them all down."

"Helpless," I said. "You're completely helpless."

After I keyed the sales into the computer, I hopped into an electric cart. The maintenance barn stood in a waste area between the eleventh and twelfth fairways and well behind the first tee. The year-round regulars on the greens crew—three Mexicans, two African-Americans, and an evangelical Christian—lounged on a circle of hay bales. They ate sandwiches from waxed-paper wrappers and, with one exception, drank beers in tiny paper bags. The six college boys hired for the summer were locked in a putting contest on the practice green. They had longish hair, lean bodies, and well-muscled arms.

My arrival caused quite a stir. The putting contest froze. The regulars looked up from their sandwiches. After a moment, everyone resumed what they were doing.

I picked my way through an obstacle course of strewn tools and tangled hoses and into the barn itself. The air closed in quickly, funky with fertilizer and sharp with chemicals. Burlap sacks lay crosswise on wooden skids, oozing trails of seed into tiny conical piles. Mats of finely cut grass, bound together by oil and moisture, clung to a set of gang mowers.

In one corner of the barn was a small office. The door was ajar, and a light glowed inside. As I padded closer, I could hear the fitful clicks of someone tapping on a computer keyboard. I stopped where I could see but not be seen. Guy Amodeo sat at the computer, a fact I'd already deduced by process of elimination. His head was tilted back and his chin jutted forward, as if he were looking at the monitor through the reading glass portion of his tinted aviator bifo-cals. The keyboard pattered, then stopped, then pattered again. I knew this cadence from observing Sam. Guy Amodeo was instant messaging.

I moved back out of sight, then noisily cleared my throat. The pattering stopped.

"Someone there?" called Guy.

"Jenny," I said.

He swung open the door without leaving his chair. At the same time, he clicked the mouse. A background minimized, leaving only a single dialog box in the middle of the screen. I knew this drill, too. Sam always hid whatever he was doing the moment I walked into the den unannounced.

"Jenny Chase," he said. "Twice in one day."

"I didn't think you noticed the first time."

"I did. Sorry for the snub. I've been preoccupied. All this now." He circled a hand in the air, encompassing the barn, or the club, maybe the world. "Charlie send you out about something?"

"No," I said. "Kit."

"She taking me up on my offer?"

His candor surprised me, so I didn't play dumb.

"I wouldn't know," I said. "Or hold my breath."

"That's not very kind." He frowned. "Too bad. I just want to help."

Right, I thought. But what I said was, "Maybe you can."

"Really?" Guy rolled back from the keyboard, exposing a waxed-paper sandwich wrapper on his lap. A soggy tomato slice and a few squiggles of lettuce stuck to the paper.

"I'm not going into a whole backstory," I said. "Let's

just say that about three weeks ago someone stuffed a letter in the Gilberts' mailbox. Kit didn't read it, but whatever it said bothered Rick enough that he called a lawyer. Did Rick say anything about it?"

"To me? Why would he?"

"You worked with him. You spent a lot of time with him. You're a guy, and guys tell other guys what they might not tell their wives. Do I need to give you another reason?"

"No, Rick didn't say anything to me about any letter." He laughed. "But how long ago did you say?"

"Three weeks. About."

Guy stroked his chin, thinking. "Three weeks ago. Maybe it was about that kid."

"What kid?"

"The girl on Soundview. Her parents sued the club because they thought this special herbicide-and-fertilizer mix Rick used a few years ago gave the girl cancer. Don't tell me you didn't know. I thought everyone did."

"Well, I didn't, but I do now. Kit told me."

"But did she tell you the girl died?" said Guy. "That was about three weeks ago."

I LUNGED AT Charlie, but he twisted out of the way.

"Let me have them," I said.

"I can't give them to you."

I lunged again. He sidestepped me.

"Why not?"

"Because I'm trusted with them."

I grabbed his arm. He quickly tossed the keys to his free hand and held them out of reach.

"You can trust me," I said.

"No, I can't. You're one of the least trustworthy people I know."

I leaped. Charlie swept the keys out of my reach with a toreador's flourish. I flew into the golf shoe department and crashed onto a chair. He came over and plopped himself down beside me. We were both huffing and puffing.

"Tell me why you need them and I'll think about it."

I explained. When I finished, we were still panting.

"Good thing nobody came in here," said Charlie. He arched his eyebrows. "They might think something happened."

"Yeah," I said. "Keep dreaming."

In the end, of course, Charlie gave me the keys. But there were conditions. He insisted on going with me, which meant that I needed to wait until we closed the shop and parked the entire fleet of carts in the barn. It was five-thirty before we trudged up to the clubhouse.

The main entrance opened into an octagonal foyer with a marble floor, crystal chandelier, vaulted ceiling, and eight grotesque plaster masks staring down from the junction where the ceiling spandrels met the engaged pilasters. Arched doorways led to the bar, two private dining rooms, and the ladies' powder room. A vending machine wrapped in dark plastic and duct tape stood against the mirrored wall between the bar and powder-room doorways. The victim of the recent vandalism, I thought.

The door to the administrative office was a hard left off the foyer. Charlie unlocked the door quietly, and we slipped inside. We may not have been trespassing, but we didn't want anyone to see us.

"I still don't understand why you're doing this," said Charlie. He opened the first of four file cabinets and began rifling through the drawer. "If Rick was despondent because the little girl died, how does that prove he didn't kill himself?"

"I didn't say he was despondent. I said he was upset."

Charlie rolled his eyes.

"You don't have kids, right?" I said. Charlie alluded to multiple ex-wives, but I'd never pinned him down to a number.

"Fatherhood is one thing I've managed to avoid."

"Then you can't possibly know the anger you would feel if someone harmed your child."

"Granted," he said. "But if this family had a motive for killing Rick because he gave their little girl cancer, how did they make it look like he killed himself?"

"That's not my problem," I said.

Charlie found the file a few minutes later. The family's name was Newman.

"Know them?" I said.

"If they aren't club members, I don't know them," he said. "Such are the boundaries of my tightly circumscribed life."

"A simple no would do," I said.

The file was thick with pleadings, deposition transcripts, and correspondence between the board of directors and the club's lawyers. We divided the file in half and began wading through.

"Look at this." Charlie passed me a transcript.

It was Rick's deposition. The first page listed the lawyers, and Rick's was none other than Roger W. Chase, Esq.

"This is a surprise," I said.

"You didn't know your husband represented Rick?" said Charlie. "Talk about circumscribed."

"We were already separated," I said. I plucked a phone off a desk and called Roger. After three rings, voice mail took over, announcing that Roger Chase was unavailable and to please leave a message.

"Roger, it's Jenny. Please call me. It's not about Sam. Bye."

AFTER CHARLIE LEFT, I strapped my bag onto a cart and rolled down to the first tee. The Open was less than two weeks away, and the thought stirred butterflies in my stomach. Tuesday's round with the girls had shown me how much I needed to get my game back together.

I locked my driver behind my spine and performed a series of isometric warm-ups. Loosened, I took some long, lazy swings and then teed up my ball. I swung. My ball traced an arc against the sky, landed dead center, and bounded toward the green.

I loved a golf course in the evening. Long shadows mixed with liquid patches of sunshine, the sky turned fuzzy, night birds warbled, sprinklers unfolded gossamer wings as they chucked softly in the distance. For me, golf was timeless and personal, and never more timeless and personal than when I played alone at dusk. My girlhood lurked out here, in lonely hollows, beyond the bend in a cart path, across quiet ponds nipped by unseen bugs. It danced ghostly on the edge of my vision, vanishing whenever I turned.

The fourth hole descends into a deep valley drained by a thin stream. I lofted a seven-iron up to the green, and as I pressed my divot back into the turf, I felt the hairs on my neck stand on end. It wasn't from the chill of a breeze or the crawl of a bug. I was being watched.

I got into the cart, my heart thumping with adrenaline. I scanned the area around the green and saw no one. Then I swung a wide turn toward the cart bridge, allowing me a quick glimpse back toward the tee. A man stood on the rim of the hill, wagging a golf club in front of him. The standing hairs rolled down my spine.

I drove into the trees, but rather than cross the cart bridge, I turned back toward the tee. Can't be, I told myself, can't be. But my thumping heart and trembling hands told me otherwise. The cart labored up the steep, rutted incline and finally broke out of the trees behind where he had been standing. But my father, if he had been my father, was gone.

I felt shaky after that but stuck to my plan of playing the first seven holes and then practicing tee shots on the eighth. Supported by a complex web of timbers and steel cables, the tee cantilevered out from the edge of a high cliff overlooking the harbor. I crossed the short grass and gripped the split-rail fence that ran around the edge. Down below, the *Maggie May* lay in its slip, buttoned up for the night.

As a golf shot, the eighth tee presented golfers with little margin for error. Charlie and I sometimes took our pupils out here for driving lessons. The fairway was tightly pinched between a line of white oaks on the right and a tumbled sea-wall curving in from the left. Beyond a ledge of bedrock and scrub grass was a tiny patch of humpbacked fairway. Land too far left, and your ball kicked over the seawall. Land too far right, and your ball skidded into the oaks. But if you popped your drive directly over the bedrock, your ball caught the downslope exactly right and rolled to the edge of a tidal pool just a flip wedge from the green.

As a prospect, few places at the club beat the eighth tee on a beautiful evening like this one. The water sparkled in the diminishing sun. A huge sailboat powered by an onshore breeze skirted the gathering of tiny green islands at the mouth of the inlet as it made for home. Way beyond, the bridges and skyscrapers of New York City revealed themselves in color, contrast, and detail as if magnified in the lens of a telescope.

I teed up and took my stance. As I looked down the fairway, my father's voice came unbidden into my head: "On a tight driving hole, you need to concentrate on a target far beyond your range. Don't look left, don't look right. Just straight ahead." Despite the earlier mirage, the voice calmed me. A mile away, a pine tree on one of the islands pointed skyward. I notched the target in my brain, put my head down, and swung.

"YES, I KNOW the Newmans on Soundview," said Danica. "They have a chocolate Lab named Trixie."

Danica's passion was dogs, and her avocation was a dog-walking business she had started as a diversion but which quickly grew into a time-consuming career. She knew the people of Poningo not by their ancestral homes or their children or their careers, but by their dogs. We were on her back deck, which overlooked the harbor and, when the leaves fell from the trees, allowed a view of the club's seventh green. I had detoured here after my driving session.

Danica sat on a chair with both knees tucked under her chin and her arms locked across her shins. She had frizzy hair and an ultralight body, and she wore extremely short cutoffs and spaghetti-string tank tops without a trace of self-consciousness. The opposite of Cindy in many ways, she got quality points for looking younger than her age. In relaxed mode now, she had taken out her contact lenses and wore tiny glasses with dark frames, a style she brought off beautifully. Her two dogs—I knew their names, but not which was which—insinuated themselves on either side of her, hoping for a slice of cheese from the block she'd pulled from the fridge when I arrived.

"Very sad about their daughter," said Danica.

"Yes," I said.

"Twelve years old. Imagine."

Down below, mist began to gather along the boat slips. The harbor was completely still, not a ripple on the water, not a jingle of bells, not a slap of ropes. Danica cut two slices of cheese. She dropped one in each dog's mouth and told them to go away. They hesitated, as if their sad faces might be worthy of another slice, then slouched off to opposite corners of the deck and lay down.

Danica cut herself a paper-thin slice, ate it, and locked her arms across her shins again.

"Why do you ask?"

"I think there might be a connection between them and Rick Gilbert," I said.

I told her about the lawsuit and my theory about the letter.

"A threat?" she said.

"That's what I'm looking for. I need something to get the police to reopen the case."

"The Newmans aren't that kind of people."

"None of us are that kind of people until the time comes."

Danica cut two more slices of cheese. A soft whistle roused the dogs. She told them to sit, then looked at each as if deciding whether they deserved the treat. After a moment, she tossed the slices. Each dog snapped one out of the air.

"The Newmans are out of town," she said. "They left about two weeks ago."

"Which day?" I said.

"I don't know. Wednesday, maybe Tuesday."

"Right around the time Rick . . ." I let my voice trail off. Danica nodded.

"Do you want to get into their house?" she said. "I walk Trixie every morning."

"I don't know what I'd be looking for."

"Then you don't know what you might find out. If you're interested, meet me there at ten."

IT WAS ALMOST full dark by the time I got back to the yard. I quickly jammed the charger cable into the battery port and forced the barn door down. I really needed to fix that kink in the track.

At my car, I sat on the edge of the open trunk and removed my golf shoes. It had been a productive day: a good practice session and a promising lead for Kit. I hoped to find something concrete tomorrow; I needed to find something concrete tomorrow. The faster I could turn evidence over to Donahue, the better prepared I'd be for the Open.

Across the parking lot, a car started up. I hadn't seen anyone go to the car, and that same sense of being watched that I'd felt on the fourth hole made a swift return, standing hairs and all. The car's lights came on, blinding me momentarily. I recovered enough to catch a glimpse of the driver's silhouette as he drove past. Could he have been the same man from the fourth hole? Maybe and maybe not. But the idea of my father watching over me at a distance was a nice thought, even if it might be miles from the truth.

FOURTEEN

TEN O'CLOCK NEVER came. Of course, it came in the "time marches on" sense, but I wasn't able to meet Danica.

I got to the club at my usual time. At eight-fifteen, my cell phone trembled. It was Sam.

"Mom, you gotta come home." He sounded scared.

"What's the matter?"

"Never mind. Just come home. Now."

I drove home fast. A police car was parked in the driveway. A uniformed cop stood at the front door, his hand raised to the brass knocker. Another man stood at the edge of the flower bed as if peering through the den window. I assumed he was a detective, because he wore jeans and a gray wind-breaker instead of a uniform. He met me on the front lawn.

"Are you Jenny Chase?" he said. He had dark hair, sharp eyes, and a bump in the middle of his nose that gave a hawkish angle to his face. In all this, he looked vaguely familiar, though I couldn't place from where.

"Yes. What's going on? My son called me."

On the stoop, the cop rattled the knocker. The man called to him and made a slashing motion.

"We're here to talk to your son," he said to me.

"About what?"

"An incident at Harbor Terrace Country Club the other night. I understand you work at the club, so you probably know about the clubhouse break-in."

Now I realized I'd seen him in front of the clubhouse when I swung around the circle yesterday morning.

"Yes, I heard about it. Why do you want to talk to Sam?"

"Find out what he knows."

"I'm sure he doesn't know a thing, Detective."

"Thanks for the promotion, ma'am, but I'm not a detective." He fixed his collar, and a silver patrolman's shield hanging from a lanyard dropped into view. "I'm Nick Cirillo, the town youth officer. I still need to talk to Sam. The easy way would be for you to go inside and explain to him it's in his best interest to talk to me."

"What's the hard way?"

"I get one of the town judges to sign a warrant."

As if on cue, the cop pounded on the door and shouted for Sam to open up. I considered my two options, easy and hard, and I wondered what Roger would do in this situation. He wanted to fight everyone, at every turn. But sometimes— and there was no rational way to predict when—he could be surprisingly accommodating. And then I flashed on Judge

Chandler, saliva drooling from his chin as he signed Sam's arrest warrant.

"I'll talk to my son," I said.

The cop stepped down from the stoop. I unlocked the door with my key but couldn't get in. Sam had hooked the security chain.

"Sam, let me in," I called through the crack.

"I don't want to see them."

"It's just me. We need to talk."

"No."

"Sam, you can't stay in there forever."

I heard some rustling. He pushed the door closed and slid back the chain. I barely got inside before he kicked the door shut. He gripped a baseball bat.

"Put that down," I said.

Sam looked at the bat as if seeing it for the first time, then leaned it beside the door. I led him into the kitchen and sat him down at the breakfast counter. I had a fleeting thought to call Roger, but then instinct took over.

"Do you know why they're here?" I said.

"No."

"There was a break-in at the clubhouse two nights ago. Somebody got inside and vandalized a vending machine. They think you know something about it."

Sam said nothing.

"Do you?"

"Sorta."

"What does that mean?"

"I was there—"

"You were what?" I said.

"Mom, will you let me finish? I was out with some kids, and we decided to skateboard at the club because the parking lot was empty and we could use the big hill."

"What kids?" I said.

"Mickey, Willy, Brian, Greg, Kieran."

"Kieran Boyle? The kid who took Judge Chandler's money?"

"Stop getting so mad, Mom. We got hungry, so we decided to go inside and buy stuff from the vending machines. But the clubhouse was closed, except one front window was open a crack. So Kieran, he's the smallest, climbed through the window to open the doors for us. Only he couldn't open the doors from the inside without a key. So more kids climbed in."

"Did you?"

Sam stared at the floor.

"Sam, did you climb in the window?"

"I kept skateboarding," he said.

It wasn't the most inspiring denial, but enough for me to relax my heightened state of alarm.

"Well, why don't we talk to the police and clear it all up," I said. "That's Officer Cirillo. He's the town youth officer."

"I know who he is, Mom. He comes to school to talk to us. How come you know so many cops lately?"

"I don't, Sam. I only know two. Officer Cirillo and Detective Donahue."

"Well, I don't want to talk to any of them."

"Sam, Officer Cirillo isn't going to go away. He probably already talked to some of the other boys and knows you were there. You need to tell your side of the story to defend yourself. Otherwise, you'll have the same problem you had with Judge Chandler's wallet."

"But, Mom—"

"Sam, sometimes you need to face your problems no matter how distasteful they might be."

Sam gave in. I opened the front door and ushered him outside. Cirillo and the cop were standing halfway down the walk. Sam's big skateboarding sneakers slapped on the stone slabs. Cirillo immediately stepped forward. "We're just going to take a little ride to the station," he said, "and talk where it's more comfortable."

Sam turned to me.

"You didn't say anything about taking him," I said.

"No, and I didn't say anything about not taking him. All the other boys went." Cirillo looked at Sam as if to imply that going to the station was an honor and that Sam would want the same treatment. "I'm not arresting Sam. We're just going someplace to talk."

"I want to come with you," I said.

"That's fine. Or you can meet us there. We can let Sam decide."

"Sam, do you want me to come with you or meet you there?"

Sam toed the grass with his sneaker. I could see he was caught between the fear of riding in a police car and the utter mortification of riding in a police car with his mother.

"Meet," he muttered.

"Okay, Sam," I said. "I'll be right behind you."

"Let's go." Cirillo clapped hands as if they were heading off to Playland.

I watched them cross the lawn to the cruiser. As Sam ducked into the backseat, he turned quickly and mouthed, "Call Dad."

INSIDE, A BAD case of the shakes overtook me. I grabbed the kitchen wall phone and managed to press in Roger's private number. He answered immediately.

"I got your message, Jenny," he said. "I was planning to call you back. Couldn't you wait?"

"Something bad just happened, Roger. The cops took Sam away."

"What?"

"Someone broke into the clubhouse and vandalized some vending machines. They want to talk to Sam."

"What the hell is going on up there?" said Roger.

"Sam was with a group of boys skateboarding at the club. Some of those boys broke in. Some didn't. He says he didn't. The cops want to find out what he knows."

"And you let them take him to the station?"

"I didn't think I had a choice."

"Of course you had a choice."

"They said all the other boys already have been down," I said. "I thought it was a good idea for Sam to tell his side of the story."

"His side of the story," Roger muttered. "And you believed them? Jenny, you never believe anything a cop tells you under these circumstances."

I wanted to tell him this wasn't just a cop; it was the town youth officer. But that would have meant nothing to Roger, and suddenly it meant nothing to me.

"Why didn't you go with Sam?" said Roger.

"He didn't want me to come. He wanted me to call you."

"Well, you did. Thanks."

"I'm going down to the station right now."

"You do that," said Roger. "And don't let Sam answer any questions. Not one. I'm going to jump on the first train and come up there."

"Good. Sam will like that."

Roger snorted derisively. "What's the police station fax number? Never mind. I'll find it myself. You get there. Tell them Sam's represented by counsel and that I'm on the way. Can you do that? Tell his side of the story. Goddammit."

CIRILLO'S OFFICE WAS in the basement, not far from a door with Donahue's name on a fake wood-grained plaque. As the desk sergeant ushered me down a corridor clogged with banks of shoulder-high file cabinets, I could see that Donahue's door was ajar and I could hear him speaking behind it. I couldn't make out the exact words, but I recognized the same soothing tones he had used on Quint Gilbert. Suddenly, that day seemed so long ago.

The office was a cop's idea of kid-friendly. Skateboard and snowboard posters hung on the walls. Video game controllers trailed away from a small TV on a side table. Rap music pounded from an MP3 player.

"Hello, Ms. Chase. We waited for you," said Cirillo. He took a legal pad from a drawer and dropped it on his desk. "What time did you get to the club that night, Sam?"

"Don't answer that," I said.

Cirillo slid back in his chair and leveled his eyes at me.

"Allowing you to sit here doesn't mean you can interrupt. You're his mother, not his lawyer."

"I don't want Sam answering any questions until his father gets here. His father is a lawyer."

"That's great. But until I hear from his father to tell me otherwise, Sam and I are free to talk. Aren't we, Sam?"

Sam grunted. I'm sure Cirillo took that as an assent, while I knew it was Sam's all-purpose noncommittal answer.

"The other boys tell me you all got there around nine. Is that right?"

"Sam," I said.

"Ms. Chase," said Cirillo.

"I don't wear a watch," said Sam.

"But you carry a cell phone. All you kids do. And they have clocks."

"I don't always look at it because it's like deep in my pocket." He wore a pair of brown bush shorts and patted the lower set of pockets for emphasis.

"Well, according to the almanac, sundown was at eight thirty-one that night," said Cirillo. "Was the sun down when you got there?"

"I really want this to stop," I said.

Cirillo turned toward me, annoyed. At that precise moment, the door opened and the sergeant handed Cirillo a fax. Cirillo read it.

"Looks like Sam is represented by counsel. Roger Chase, Esquire. We need to sit tight till he gets here."

Cirillo looked at me accusingly, as if I'd conjured the fax out of the ether. Then he got up and left the office. I exhaled deeply.

"Your father's on the way." I turned down the volume on the MP3 player. "He'll know what to do."

"He always does," said Sam.

There were times his most innocent statements sounded like accusations. This was one of them.

"Sam, are you telling me the truth? Were you more involved than you're saying?"

"Dad wouldn't want me to talk."

"I'm your mother, Sam."

"Yeah, but the room might be bugged."

HALF AN HOUR later, Roger blew into the office. He slammed his briefcase onto Cirillo's desk, then raked his fingers back through his dark, curly hair. After a frozen moment of what I took to be some process of mental reorientation, Roger opened his briefcase and arrayed several soft-covered law books in front of him.

"I need to confer with my client alone," he said. He looked neither at me nor at Sam but sidelong into the space between us.

"Don't be ridiculous, Roger."

"The attorney-client privilege is one of the most sacred tenets in the law," he said. "It vanishes once a third party is present."

"I'm not a third party. I'm his mother." I seemed to be reminding everyone of this fact.

"Mom," said Sam.

"Okay, okay, I'm leaving."

In a deeply psychological move, I went straight to Donahue's office.

"What are you doing here?" he said.

I sat down before I answered.

"Officer Cirillo brought Sam in," I said. "He wanted to question Sam about some vandalism at the club."

"I'm sorry," said Donahue. His sleeves were rolled up neatly, the plastic bracelets hanging together on his wrists. An oscillating fan sat on the floor beside the desk. Its air current washed across me, raising goose bumps on my arms.

"My ex is here, too, as Sam's lawyer."

"I see." Donahue mulled that over for a moment. "I heard about that incident. Some people take a 'boys will be boys' attitude toward minor incidents. Not Nick. His theory is you sweat the minor stuff and the major stuff never gets a chance to happen. I'm sorry Sam's involved."

"He says he isn't," I said. "He says he was there, which I believe, but that he didn't do anything, which I'm not sure I believe."

"The truth usually wins out in these things. It really does."

I glanced around the office. On the walls were the predictable plaques and certificates, with words like "Youth Bureau" and "DARE." On his credenza stood a framed photo of him and his son at the town dock. I never saw the boy up close that day at the dock, and from the picture it was obvious he hadn't inherited his father's height and physique. He had the body, if I could be so unkind, of a harbor seal.

Donahue tapped a pencil on his desk. "Any progress in your investigation?" he said.

"I can't think about that right now."

I instantly regretted what I said. The state I was in wasn't Donahue's fault.

"Well, just so you know, I haven't archived the file yet."

"Anything I said?"

"No. Just being cautious."

"Actually, I do have a lead," I said. "At least I think it's a lead. I haven't had a chance to look into it. Who knows now if I ever will."

"Details?" He grinned expectantly.

"I don't have any yet. All I can say is that there could be a revenge aspect. Somebody may have wanted to get back at Rick for hurting a child."

"Whose child?"

"I can't say. I won't say."

"You need to keep me posted on this," Donahue said seriously.

"Don't worry," I said.

FIFTEEN

"I'M NOT GETTING the whole story," said Roger.

We had hit the sidewalk outside the police station and were heading toward town. Our unspoken destination, I divined, was Chang's Luncheonette.

"From whom?" I said.

"Either of them. Maybe both. Probably both."

Sam walked up ahead of us, hands in his pockets and shoulders hunched, his big skateboarding sneakers scuffing the ground. I touched Roger's arm and pressed a finger to my lips. Even though Sam was several yards away, his teenage ears could pick up our conversation like a high-tech listening device.

"How well do you know this Cirillo?" Roger spoke several decibels lower.

"I just met him today. All I know is that he's the town youth officer."

"He's not treating this as simple vandalism. He's speaking in terms of burglary."

"Which means?" I didn't want to mention what Donahue told me about Cirillo's philosophy. The habit of not telling Roger any more than he asked was deeply ingrained.

"That's a felony. It's a much more serious charge."

"What did Sam tell you?"

"Same thing that he told you," said Roger. "He was there, but he didn't go into the clubhouse."

I felt myself smirk. "Maybe that's what happened."

"Maybe it is. But we're in a different realm if this goes to court. It's not about what actually happened. It's about what can be proven to have happened."

Up ahead, Sam stopped at the corner of Poningo and Elm. The light was against him. Roger and I stopped, too, staying out of earshot.

"Cirillo has some kind of evidence against Sam," said Roger. "It's the only thing that makes any sense."

"Isn't he supposed to tell you?"

"Eventually, but not yet."

At Chang's, all discussion of Sam's predicament ceased. Sam and I slid into one side of a booth, Roger opposite. A waitress poured coffee into two thick brown mugs and took our orders. Coffee turned Roger expansive, and after a few sips he leaned back and stretched his arms across the booth.

"So why the call last night?" he said.

I quickly war-gamed a conversation in my head. If I told him about my investigation, he would draw the conclusion— and not necessarily an erroneous one—that I was trying to solve someone else's problem while a more important one developed under my own roof. He might not say anything now, but he would tuck it away and use it against me later. So I made up a story about running across the deposition transcripts while helping Charlie look for something in the administrative office.

"I didn't know you represented Rick Gilbert," I said.

"Well, I did." Roger darkened at the thought but took another sip of coffee and brightened almost instantly.

"That damn board," he said. "They expected Rick to eradicate that weed, then refused to defend him when he was sued. The bastards. It was just another reason I left the club."

I, of course, was the main reason.

"That was a tense deposition," said Roger. "Mr. Newman sat in to listen. Even his own lawyer didn't like the idea, but a party has the right to attend all the depositions in a case. Newman wanted to break the club financially and he wanted to break Rick psychologically. Every time Rick began to answer a question, Newman taunted him, called him a liar, a child abuser. It was horrible, a deposition I'll never forget as long as I practice. And Rick was so sincere. He never intended to hurt anyone. He researched the risks of those chemicals to the best of his ability. He truly believed they were safe. He was shocked by Newman's venom. I tried to get the judge to bar Newman from the deposition, but she refused. So we pressed forward. The deposition should have taken a day. With all the interruptions and tirades and calls to the judge for rulings, it took four."

"So it's safe to say Mr. Newman hated Rick," I said.

Roger put down his mug and leveled his eyes at me. He obviously wondered why I asked that question in that way, which sounded remarkably like one of his leading questions to a witness at a trial.

"I'd say so," he said. "Why?"

"The Newman girl died about three weeks ago."

"Oh, my God." Roger lifted the mug but didn't bring it to his mouth. He stared into the middle distance. Beside me, Sam picked at a crack in the Formica. I poked his ribs.

"There was no proof," said Roger. "Zero. Nil. Zilch. We think we know why things happen. *Propter hoc, ergo hoc.*" He looked at Sam. "That's Latin. It means 'After this, then because of this.'"

Sam squirmed. Roger insisted that he take Latin come September, and today my fond hope was that he would be taking it at Poningo High School and not a juvenile detention center.

"Sometimes those reasons make sense," Roger continued. "And sometimes they may even be the truth. But to prove those reasons in a court of law can be difficult."

"When was the last time you spoke to Rick?"

"A long time. Years."

"He called me the night before he died," I said.

"About what?"

"I don't know. I didn't speak to him. I saw a strange number logged on the caller ID. I thought it was . . . never mind who I thought it was . . . and when I called it back, the detective answered as he vouchered Rick's cell phone."

"Amazing," said Roger.

"I can't think of any reason for him to call me, unless he wanted to contact you."

"Why do you think he wanted to contact me?"

"Well, his wife told me he tried to contact other lawyers a few weeks ago. About what, she didn't know."

"About the Newman girl?" said Roger.

"The timing makes sense."

Roger wiped his mouth and crumpled his napkin. "If he did try to call me at the office, he wouldn't have gotten through. He's on my PNG list. Persona non grata." I expected him to look at Sam, but he didn't. "My secretary keeps the list by her phone. It changes daily, but Rick was a permanent member."

"Why weren't you talking to him?" I said.

"I won that case for him. I didn't charge him a dime. And you know what? I never even got a thank-you."

The food came, and with it a change of tone, mood, and subject. Namely, money. Ever since I quit teaching we had a running argument about my income, which was one factor in the mathematical calculation of Roger's monthly child support nut. Unlike most divorced women, who hid or minimized their income, I took the opposite tack. I lied. I told Roger that what I lost in salary I made up in lesson fees. I did this not to deny Sam his rightful support or because I had some death wish desire to strain an already tight budget. I just wanted to keep the important things, like custody, as they were.

"How do you plan to finance the Open?" said Roger.

"I'm not financing it," I said. "I'm playing in it. And thanks for the congratulations."

Roger speared a hunk of bacon and folded it into his mouth.

"Driving, living on cold cuts and white bread, hiring a cut-rate caddie." I nodded at Sam.

"Your father had an appointment with me yesterday," said Roger. "He and a group of investors want to build a chain of all-weather, all-season golf ranges between here and the Rust Belt. I'm handling the legal end."

"Cute," I said. Roger knew it was a word I didn't often use in complimentary fashion.

"He knows you qualified, and he wondered whether he should offer to pay your air fare and hotel accommodations." Roger waited a beat for a reaction. "I told him you were too proud."

"I am." I quickly gulped down the last cold slug of coffee in my mug. "Besides, I'm driving because I may not come back right away. I just might qualify for the next tournament and who knows how many after that."

"Really?" said Roger. "That would open a new round of discussion between us."

Roger enjoyed his verbal feints and jukes and said not another word on that subject. I left Chang's vaguely troubled. It wasn't about Sam; I already knew that if I ever won a permanent place on the tour, I'd have a custody battle on my hands. No, I was troubled about the proximity of my father and his attorney-client relationship with Roger. The idea that he was a ghostly image watching me from afar was comforting. The truth that he was close and refused contact was a kick in the gut.

NIGHT HAD FALLEN. An army had massed outside, laying siege.

"Why not?" said Sam. He had his skateboard under one arm and a baseball cap fixed backward on his head.

This was the dilemma I'd been wrestling with all day. Sam hadn't been arrested or charged with any crime. Yet. But he was officially in trouble, with Roger predicting in his darkly nebulous way that there would be serious court proceedings in the offing. That was Roger's problem; my dilemma was how to handle Sam in the meantime. My immediate reaction was to ground him. The idea wasn't punishment for the sins of the past but to protect him from the temptations of the future. He wasn't seeing the distinction.

"Because," I said.

"Because isn't a good reason," he said, quoting one of my own stock lines.

Outside, the army began to rumble, and then the rumble resolved into shouting Sam's name.

"Okay," I said. "You can go out with the boys. But you are back in this house at ten o'clock." His jaw dropped at the nerve—the nerve—of such an early curfew. "And you are to call me every half hour to tell me where you are and what you are doing."

"Every half hour?"

"Set the alarm on your phone. If you're embarrassed to call your mother in front of your friends, sneak off and do it alone. If you don't call, I'll call you. If I need to call you, I knock a half hour off your curfew. And if I don't reach you, I'll come find you. And I will find you."

"Fine," said Sam.

I watched through the window. The boys high-fived and punched shoulders and skated circles around the pavement in front of the house before shooting down the block. I didn't know how I would find Sam if he didn't answer his phone. But I needed him to think I still had a few parental superpowers at my disposal.

SIXTEEN

AT FIVE MINUTES to ten the next morning, I crossed the golf course in an electric cart. Soundview ran between the second and eleventh holes, the road descending toward the harbor in a series of natural terraces that gave the club its name. Halfway up the eleventh fairway, a dirt path wide enough for a set of gang mowers cut between two houses, stopped at the road, then picked up again at the other side. The Newmans lived in a house abutting the path.

I stashed the cart in a hollow alongside a stone wall and spotted Danica heading up from below on Soundview. Her two dogs strained at their leashes.

Danica had called me last night smack between two calls from Sam, who earned a fifteen-minute curfew extension for reporting in as scheduled.

"Where were you?" she'd said.

"Something came up."

"I'm sure. You were spotted at Chang's with Roger."

"We needed to discuss something."

"Hmm. Well, the Newmans return tomorrow night. If you still need to get inside, meet me at ten."

So here it was, ten A.M., and Danica was on time. She lashed her leashes to the stair rail, scooped the day's mail from the mailbox, and unlocked the front door. Inside, a dog charged into the foyer, panting and wagging its tail. It was a chocolate Lab, I think. It jumped up on Danica, who squeezed its jaw and smacked an air kiss beside its face. Then it came after me. I turned sideways, a trick Danica had taught me to dissuade dogs from showing me unwanted affection. With nowhere to jump, it nosed my hand, which I immediately shoved into a pocket.

Danica flipped through the mail, actually holding up an envelope to the light.

"Remind me never to have you walk my dog," I said.

"Number one, you'll never get a dog," she said. "Number two, these people open their lives to me."

"But not their mail."

Danica smiled at something she evidently saw through the envelope, then dropped that letter and the rest of the mail into a large basket on a side table.

"Come with me," she said.

I followed her through a living room and into a small den. A computer table stood between two windows that looked across a hedgerow of ragged forsythia into the windows of the neighboring house.

"Mr. Newman leaves his computer on twenty-four

seven," said Danica, and indeed the moment she spoke, I detected a hum coming from the tower beneath the computer table.

Danica swirled the mouse, and the screen brightened with the crackle of roused electrons.

"He has two word-processing programs." She touched the cursor to each of the icons.

"I'm afraid to ask how you know this," I said.

"I'll be about twenty minutes with Trixie," she said, breezing past my comment. "The gardeners come today, just in case you hear a commotion."

"Thanks. I'll be fine." I sat down and opened one of the word-processing programs. In the distance, Danica closed the front door. The lock clicked into place.

Most of the files were letters, and most of the letters were conveniently named and numbered to create lines of correspondence on particular topics. Many of these letters were addressed to the Newmans' medical insurer, asking for preapproval of different medical procedures for their daughter. Her name, I discovered now, was Amanda. The letters were tersely eloquent; many were tartly polite. Each one wrapped words around a core of resolve. These parents would do anything for their daughter. I wondered how far "anything" would go.

I closed out the first program and opened the second. I found more letters, but none related to Amanda, her illness, or the lawsuit. Then, in a subdirectory labeled "MISC," I found a file called "CHRON." It was a detailed chronology running back to that date four years ago when Rick first applied his herbicide-fertilizer mix to the golf course.

HORRIBLE SMELL. WOKE AMANDA UP DURING
THE NIGHT. SHE SLEPT WITH US. WINDOWS
CLOSED.

Several more entries described the smell ("like dirty socks
and turpentine"), the blue mist hanging over the golf course
in the mornings ("like gunsmoke over Gettysburg"), the
withering of a patch of impatiens in the backyard garden,
and the blistering of paint on the side of the house facing
the prevailing southwesterly breeze.

Then, in December, the first symptoms appeared.

AMANDA FATIGUED LATELY. IN BED BY EIGHT
O'CLOCK. NOT LIKE HER.

SPONTANEOUS BRUISING ON AMANDA'S ARMS.
SAYS SHE DOESN'T REMEMBER BANGING THEM.

WOKE UP SCREAMING. PILLOW SATURATED
WITH BLOOD. NOSEBLEED.

I scrolled down, skimming over details because I knew
lingering would bring tears to my eyes. I was looking for
mention of Rick, and there was no mention of Rick. The
chronology was clinical, impersonal. It ended at the filing
of the lawsuit.

I closed out the program and sat back in the chair. The
computer was the wrong place to look. Someone who was
angry enough to kill wouldn't likely sit before the cool,
buzzing electrons of a computer to vent his rage by tapping

on a keyboard. He would more likely use pen, pencil, or a blood-red crayon to etch his anger physically onto the page.

I left the den and wandered up to the second floor. Amanda's room had the feel of a life preserved. Lace curtains hung on the windows, dividing the morning sunlight into geometric patterns that trembled on the Early American comforter stretched on the bed. On the floor beside the bed were three arrangements of American Girl dolls: One sat at a student desk, her hand raised; another, in jodhpurs and riding helmet, brushed a horse's mane; the third, bundled in an Eskimo parka, sat on a toboggan pulled by a tiny husky.

I stepped around the dolls to the window and parted the curtains. Down below, in the backyard, were a stack of patio chairs, a table with a tattered plastic tablecloth, an empty flower bed. Through an opening in the trees, the clubhouse tower rose on the hill.

I backed away from the window. On the wall nearby was a framed photo of the three Newmans in front of Sleeping Beauty's castle at Disney World. The year was printed in gold in the lower left corner, but I didn't need to see the year to know that Amanda already was sick. I could see it in her face. Oh, she was smiling all right. What ten-year-old girl wouldn't smile standing between Mommy and Daddy in that iconic setting? But her eyes seemed to have separated themselves from the rest of the photo, staring distantly beyond the camera at what she must have known in her little heart was going to happen. At that moment, *I* could have killed Rick Gilbert.

The doorbell startled me. For a second, I thought it was Danica. Twenty minutes had to have passed. But why would she ring the bell? Why not just open the door and let in the dog?

Another ring. I'd never heard this doorbell before, but I could sense impatience, as if someone were jabbing at the button. I left Amanda's bedroom. A hallway ran from front to back on the second floor, and a window at the end looked down over the front door. Danica had mentioned the gardener. Perhaps he was asking what needed to be done. But when I parted the curtain, I didn't see any gardener's truck. I saw a police car.

The doorbell rang a third time. As I looked down, the cop stepped back from the front door and looked up.

I jumped back from the window. Two distinct emotions surged through me. The first was a cold, knee-wobbling fear. I leaned against the wall, wondering if I would faint and thinking that if I did, Charlie wouldn't be there to catch me. Then the second emotion, panic, rolled in and stiffened me with a good old-fashioned shot of adrenaline. I whipped out my cell phone and called Danica.

"Where are you?" I said.

"I don't know. Trixie ran, my dogs took off after her. I'm somewhere past the golf course in the high weeds near the water."

"A cop's outside. He rang the doorbell three times, and now he's looking in one of the front windows."

"Oh shit," said Danica. "I knew it."

"Knew what?"

"I should have closed the curtains in the den. The lady next door, she's kind of nosy. She probably saw you through the window and called the cops."

"Great," I said. "Now what do I do?"

"Sit tight."

The doorbell rang again, and then the latch rattled.

"Sit tight?" I said. "He's trying to get in the front door."

"Relax. I locked it. Hold on."

Danica's voice faded into a hiss of rustling and scratching. I edged closer to the window. The cop had stepped down the stairs again and stood with his arms akimbo, appraising the house. Then, as if hit by an idea, he walked around the side.

Danica returned.

"I'll get there as fast as I can. Try not to get spotted."

Something rattled downstairs. A window? A door?

"I think he's trying to get in. Listen." I held out the phone. As if on cue, something else rattled. "Hear that?"

"I heard it," said Danica. "I'm running now."

"Hurry," I said. "What if he comes in?"

"Hide. See you."

I closed my phone and shoved it into my pocket. Danica'd better run like hell. And she'd better be thinking about some logical explanation for the cop because he wasn't going away any time soon. Another rattle. He was checking all the windows, probably looking for signs of a forced entry.

I held my breath, steadied myself by gripping the top of the stairway railing. The next rattle was slightly deeper in pitch, more like a door than a window. There was a brief pause, then a click and a slow creaking sound. I felt a subtle change in air pressure.

"Hello?" came a voice. "Police."

He was in the house! I could hear deliberate footsteps. He was crossing the kitchen floor. Possibly with his gun drawn.

"Police. Anyone here?"

Closer now. I needed to do something. Fast. I padded into Amanda's room and crawled under the bed. Not the most clever hiding place, but I didn't expect to outsmart him; my only hope was to delay until Danica arrived.

The cop called out one more time. I could tell from his voice that he was at the bottom of the stairs. I expected to hear footfalls, but several seconds of total silence passed. Then I heard static.

"Post twelve," he said, barely above a whisper. "I'm at Five Four Soundview. Possible home intrusion. Need backup."

I lifted the bed skirt and looked out. The American Girl student had toppled off her chair. I must have brushed her as I went past. I could see the top of the stairs. The radio static was gone; I heard no footfalls. That doll was the only thing out of place in the room, and if the cop saw it, he would know I was near. I pushed myself forward, shot my hand under the bed skirt, and righted the doll.

Down below, the cop started up the stairs. Here we go, I thought. It was only a question of time before he looked under the bed and found me. I couldn't get away, couldn't phone Roger for help after I didn't get away. Even if I explained what I was doing in the house, even if Danica confirmed every syllable of my story, the simple fact was that I was in someone's house without permission. It would be the end of my life as an upstanding citizen, and worse, the end of Sam living with me. Because once Roger got hold of this one, he'd never let go until he won a change of custody. I could curse Rick Gilbert, but I knew I had no one to blame but myself.

The creaking footfalls slowly ascended the stairs. I laid my head sideways, one eye peering beneath the edge of the bed skirt. Through the doorway, the spindles of the balustrade stood like the bars of a jail cell along the edge of the stairwell. Any second now, the cop's head would crest above the floor.

All at once, there was a commotion. The click of a lock, the snap of an opening door, the jingle of metal, the skitter of dog toenails on hardwood.

"Hello," called Danica.

She made it. I never expected her to make it. But here she was.

The cop must have retreated down the stairs. I could hear them talking in the hallway, Danica identifying herself as the dog walker, the cop explaining why he was here, Danica responding that the neighbor must have been mistaken. I could tell from their voices that Danica was drawing the cop toward the front door, trying to lead him outside. Brilliant girl.

I pulled myself out from under the bed and lay on the carpet beside the doll with the Eskimo parka. Danica chattered on. Yes, she was the person at the computer, she was saying. The man of the house was having problems with his Internet connection, and she checked the computer each day to make sure the settings were correct. The cop wasn't saying anything. He was either buying this preposterous story or simply couldn't get a word in over Danica. I felt the front door open and close. And then the direction of Danica's voice changed, coming not up the stairs, but in through the front window.

I pushed myself upright and tiptoed to the hallway window. Down below, Danica still chattered like crazy. She had chased the cop halfway to his patrol car.

This was my chance. I padded down the stairs and landed gently on the hall floor. I was safe as long as Danica was talking. The back door was off the kitchen and luckily faced away from the neighbor's house. The door was open—this was how the cop got in—and I slipped out quietly.

I didn't run. Running was an admission of guilt, and now that I was outside rather than cowering beneath the bed while a cop searched the house, what I had done didn't seem quite so terrible. I crossed the backyard. A low stone wall separated the yard from the path. I swung my legs over. The electric cart was just a few feet away. Beyond the end of the path, a foursome tooled up the eleventh fairway. I jumped into the cart, jammed the key into the ignition switch. In a few seconds, I'd be gone. I'd get back to the pro shop, settle myself down, then phone Danica on her cell and thank her profusely.

"Hold it!"

I turned. A cop was picking his way through the saplings and weeds that grew along the section of stone wall separating the golf course from the yard. At first, I wondered how Danica's cop could have gotten back there so fast.

Then I realized he wasn't Danica's cop. He was a different cop, and in fact, he was Nick Cirillo.

Cirillo came up to the cart and raised a foot onto the front bumper. He was in uniform rather than plainclothes, and burrs were stuck to his pants.

"Did I just see you come out of that yard?" he said.

I turned back toward the house as if I needed to see what he was talking about.

"I came from that way." I pointed toward the other end of the path.

"Funny," he said. "We got a call about an intruder in that house. I could have sworn I saw someone climb over that wall."

"Wasn't me," I said.

"Ten, this is twelve," crackled Cirillo's radio. "What's your position?"

Cirillo took his foot off the bumper and stepped back.

"Ten here. Behind the house."

"I have the dog walker here. She says she was in the house. Neighbor's not sure what she saw now. House is clean. You got anything?"

Cirillo turned away from the radio and stared at me.

"Ten, you there?"

"Yeah," said Cirillo. "I got nothing."

"Out," said the other cop.

Cirillo came back to the cart and set his foot on the dashboard. I took a chance and pinched a burr off his cuff.

"Where are you headed?" he said.

I flicked the burr toward the eleventh fairway. "That way. Back to the pro shop."

"Keep your eyes open," he said. "If you see anyone who looks suspicious, let me know."

He stepped back from the cart. I turned the ignition, and the electric motor whined.

"I'll be sure to scream," I told him.

SEVENTEEN

FOR THE NEXT three days, I saw Cirillo everywhere. At the A&P he was in the produce aisle, squeezing avocados. At the Citgo station he was at the self-serve island, wiping his windshield with a squeegee. At the library he was at the reference desk, speaking deeply to a pretty research assistant with blond hair and big *Where's Waldo?* eyeglasses. He caught my eye at each of these chance meetings, the pure chance of all of them becoming decreasingly likely, and mugged as if to say, "Funny meeting you here again."

I took to driving with one eye in the rearview mirror and almost broadsided a delivery truck on Poningo Street. Finally, at dusk on the third day, I pulled into my driveway after dropping Sam at a friend's house and saw an unmarked sedan parked opposite. This was too much. I slammed my car door and crossed the street.

Cirillo stared straight forward, his head bobbing from

side to side. If he didn't actually see me, he was doing a fine job of pretending to ignore me. I thumped the window glass. He rolled it down and plucked earbuds from his ears.

"If you're going to follow me," I said, "the least you could do is come to the front door like a proper visitor."

I was at my front steps when I heard his car door open and close.

He sat in one of the big chairs on the screened-in porch while I poured iced tea in the kitchen. My iced tea isn't a suspension of chemical crystals in cold water. I make it from scratch, with tea bags and lemons and sugar and a dash of salt.

The ice cubes tinkled as I set the glasses on the table. Cirillo leaned back. He'd been looking at the books in the lawyer's bookcase.

"Where's Sam?" he said.

"At a friend's house." I sat down. "So why are you following me?"

"I'm not. I've always been around. You've just started noticing me."

"Like you noticed the librarian?"

"Oh, her?" Cirillo shrugged and took a quick sip. "An old friend."

I smirked. Cirillo was the type of self-consciously handsome guy who had women on the hook all over town. Or liked to think he did.

"I'm curious," he said. "Why were you in that house on Soundview?"

"I told you, I wasn't."

"Don't get so defensive."

"You're accusing me of a crime. How else do you expect me to be?"

"Well, it's going no further. No complaint from the home owners. Case closed. Satisfied?"

I nodded.

"So hypothetically speaking," he said, "why would you have been in that house?"

"Why are you so set on prosecuting Sam?"

"Just doing my job, ma'am."

"It's Jenny," I said.

"Okay, then, Jenny." Cirillo lifted his glass in salute. "I'm doing my job. I try to do it well so I won't be doing it forever. Right now, I'm still a cop and part-time youth officer. I don't get an extra dime in my paycheck for YO, just the hope that it will help me make detective. That's how Donahue did it. That's how I hope to do it. And just to be clear, I investigate. It's the local assistant district attorney who prosecutes."

"What are you investigating here?"

"I'm not sure."

He held my eye for a long moment, and I didn't break away. He was younger than me, though not by many years, which made him too old to have been a patrolman for very long. He must have had another career.

"To answer your question," I said, "I'm trying to help a widow with a problem. If I had been in that house, which I wasn't, I would have been looking for evidence that a certain event didn't happen the way everyone assumes it did."

"Would that event have been a suicide?"

"It might have been," I said.

"And would the evidence you hypothetically were looking for show that someone might have had a motive for harming this hypothetical suicide?"

"Hypothetically."

Cirillo leaned toward the bookcase. "You into Shakespeare?" he said.

"Remnants of a former life. I taught English lit for ten years, then went back to my golf career. I still do the occasional guest lecture."

"High school?"

"College. Manhattanville."

"Cool." He leaned back, and when he did it was as if he had completely shut Shakespeare out of his mind. "But I'm tired of talking hypothetically. I want to talk about specifics."

"Like what?"

"Like you." He took a deep breath. "We have a small department. When Donahue heard about the suspected intruder in the house on Soundview, he brought me into his office to debrief me. When I mentioned you, it was like a bell went off in his head. He asked me to look into the Newmans' movements around the time of Rick Gilbert's death. They were out of town."

"Oh," I said.

The phone rang. I excused myself and went into the kitchen to answer. I could see Cirillo through the doorway. He opened the bookcase doors and ran a finger along the spines. Then he leaned back in the chair and looked around the porch, no doubt logging details with his detective-in-training eye so he could understand in his detective-in-training mind why a fortyish college professor turned golf pro would enter someone's house to investigate an incident no one believed to be a crime. Well, if Donahue was asking Cirillo to look into this, maybe he was more interested in Rick Gilbert than I thought. My only hope was that the caller was Danica. I wanted to lambaste her.

But life isn't so neatly orchestrated. It was Roger.

"Is Sam home?" he said.

"Hello, Roger. No."

"Good. I want to explain to you what's going on so you can prepare him. There's going to be a felony hearing in town court on Thursday."

"What's a felony hearing?"

"Sam's been formally charged with a felony. Burglary three."

"No one told me."

"That's because they told me. There are two ways to proceed. Grand jury indictment or felony hearing. I requested the hearing."

"I'm sure you have a good reason."

"I have three," said Roger. "One, Sam gets to defend himself at a hearing. He doesn't in a grand jury. Two, the hearing will be before Henry Chandler."

"But he hates Sam," I cut in.

"I'm aware of that. But Henry and I go way back, and I know I can intimidate him. Three, the assistant district attorneys assigned to small-town courts like Poningo aren't as experienced as the ones assigned to grand jury. I win the hearing, and the case is over."

"And if you lose?"

"The case goes on, possibly to trial, probably to some kind of deal."

"Okay." I peeked through the doorway. Cirillo had taken a book from the shelf and was paging through it.

"Where is Sam?" said Roger. "Not gallivanting, I hope."

"At a friend's house. He checks in with me every hour. It's my new rule with him, and he's following it."

"Good," he said, but without any conviction. "I need you to get Sam ready for Thursday. He needs to look presentable. A haircut would help. The hearing's at ten. I'll be at the house by eight. I'll need to prepare him."

Roger rang off. I hung up the phone and pressed my forehead against the wall. Courtrooms were Roger's world the way a golf course was mine. He saw this hearing in terms of strategy, argument, and counterargument. I saw it as my baby's first step on the road to prison.

Roger was in control, and all I could do was stand by helplessly, maybe get Sam a haircut. But maybe not. After all, Sam's arresting officer was sitting on my porch for reasons that suddenly made no sense.

I pushed back from the wall. Fluffed my hair. Arranged my blouse. Straightened my slacks. But when I went to the porch, Cirillo was gone.

THE NEXT MORNING, I woke up in a different frame of mind. All my problems were still here—Sam, Kit Gilbert, and the Open—but they now crossed the stage of my mind against a backdrop of optimism. I wasn't sure whether it was because this cup (the investigation) had been taken from me or because something happened with Cirillo last night that I didn't quite understand but somehow boded well for the future.

Today was my late day on the schedule, so I drove Sam to the club. He knew all about the hearing because Roger, ever the impatient one, had called him on his cell immediately after talking to me. Roger apparently had described his strategy in military terms. He would draw the attacking army (the ADA and his minions) into a crossfire (cross-examination). According to Sam, this was a strategy used by "some Civil War general or maybe a Revolutionary War general." I sighed.

"Did your father say anything else?"

Sam looked at me quizzically.

"Did he mention getting a haircut?"

"What?"

Obviously, Roger had left that part of his grand strategy to me. The rest of the ride to the club devolved into haggling over millimeters.

In the quiet back at home, I tried to recapture my wake-up mood. I wanted to grasp it and analyze it, but it kept squirting to the periphery. I made myself a cup of tea and phoned Danica. I caught her on a dog walk.

"Did you know that the Newmans were out of town the day Rick Gilbert died?"

"What day was that?"

I told her.

"I have my book. Hold on." Danica recorded all of her walking jobs in a tiny memo pad. "You know, that's right."

"So why did you suggest that I look in their house?"

"You were so convincing that night you came over. I

thought maybe the Newmans took the trip as a cover. You know, maybe they left the house but stayed in the area."

"I'm the one who should be grasping at straws," I said. "Not you."

Well, that felt better, I thought after I hung up. Maybe the wake-up mood was more about the end of the investigation than it was about Cirillo. I needed to see Kit soon, preferably today. I'd tell her that my theory had been disproved and that I had no other theory to pursue. That's what I would do.

The doorbell rang.

I found two cops at the doorstep. Several yards behind them, Cirillo stood on the walk. He wore jeans and a windbreaker, his hands thrust into his pockets. Youth officer mode.

"Ms. Chase," said one of the cops, "we have a search warrant we need to execute."

He handed me a single piece of paper stapled to a blue legal back. I quickly read down to the blank space where someone had printed "one pair of Jake Reed skateboarding sneakers." The warrant was signed by Judge Henry Chandler.

"If you would step aside," the cop said.

"Hold it." Cirillo climbed onto the stoop and motioned for the cops to step down. He spoke softly. "Jenny, I'm very sorry about this."

"What's it all about?" I said.

"Just what it says. We need those sneakers."

"I thought you didn't prosecute."

"I don't. This is the DA's request. I don't even need to be

here. I tagged along because I didn't want these guys tearing up your house."

"Am I supposed to thank you?"

"You could," he said. "And you could hand over the sneakers. It would make this easier for everyone."

And so I did. I found them on opposite sides of Sam's bedroom with yesterday's smelly socks stuffed into them. The stitching along the toes was split and the laces had snapped and been retied in several places. They were barely a month old.

I carried the sneakers downstairs. The police had shifted back into their original formation, the cops on the stoop and Cirillo several paces back on the walk. One of the cops held open a clear plastic bag with the word *EVI-DENCE* printed on it. I dropped the sneakers inside.

The two cops backed off the stoop and passed Cirillo on the walk. Cirillo wore a pained expression, a mix of embarrassment and apology. He started to speak, but I closed the door in his face.

I went right to the phone and called Roger on his private line.

"The cops were just here with a search warrant," I said.

"What did they take?"

"Sam's skateboarding sneakers."

"Was he wearing them that night?"

"I assume so. He was skateboarding," I said. "And the very next day, I saw the cops looking closely at the ground below the window. It didn't mean anything to me at the time...."

"Damn," said Roger, and hung up.

EIGHTEEN

"ROGER CALLED," CHARLIE said as soon as I walked into the shop. "He wants you to call him back ASAP."

I did. It turned out that Roger had heard my last words of our conversation and, having had time to think, now gave me rapid-fire instructions. I wrote them down on a piece of paper. Charlie watched in silence.

"Problems?" he said when I hung up the phone.

"Big ones," I said. "This isn't between Roger and me, though I wish it were."

I told Charlie about Roger's plan to defend Sam at a felony hearing and my surprise visit from the cops with the search warrant for Sam's skateboarding sneakers. Charlie listened closely, then picked up my list.

"Pix, measurements, soft slash soil?"

"That means softness of soil," I said. "He means in the flower bed."

"Did he say why he needed all this?"

"Not specifically. I still get my hackles up when he starts barking orders. I doubt that will ever go away."

Without another word, Charlie walked into the bag room and returned with a tape measure. Then he opened a drawer and lifted a box containing a digital camera onto the counter. The ends of the box were still sealed with the original packing tape.

"I bought it last Christmas. I thought it would be a good teaching tool. You know, take photos of swings and put them on a computer screen." He smiled. "Of course, I don't know how to use the damn thing."

It took me all of five minutes to get the camera working.

The yard was quiet. Only a few caddies slouched on the benches beneath the lilacs. Sam, apparently, was out on the golf course.

"We'll be back in five minutes," Charlie shouted across to Eddie-O as we started up the hill.

"You're miffed," Charlie said as he stretched the tape to measure the distance from the base of the clubhouse wall to the edge of the flower bed.

"It's his attitude," I said. "You'd think we could pull together at a time like this."

"You have, haven't you?"

Scowling, I took the tape measure inside, opened the powder-room window, and played out enough tape for Charlie to grab it. He called out the measurements, first from the windowsill to the ground below and then from the windowsill out to the edge of the flower bed. I wrote down the numbers.

"Roger's a good lawyer," Charlie said. "He knows what he's doing. If you ask me, he wants to prove Sam couldn't have climbed in through the window."

Charlie often took Roger's side during our frequent tiffs. I wasn't sure if this was some form of male solidarity or reverse psychology to improve his standing with me.

"But I need to know," I said. "I don't like being kept in the dark."

"That's what makes you you," said Charlie.

I retracted the tape and went outside and took a bunch of pictures. Charlie stayed out of my way till I finished. I handed him the camera and walked through the flower bed, bouncing with each step to feel the soil underfoot. It gave as easily as low-tide sand but didn't fall into itself after I lifted my foot away. Looking back after reaching the grass, I saw a trail of well-defined footprints.

"Do you know where Kit is?" I said.

We were walking back down the hill, and I could see that the Volvo wasn't parked outside the cottage.

"Not a clue," said Charlie.

"I need to talk to her. I need to tell her I can't help her anymore and if she wants to prove Rick didn't kill himself, she needs to hire a private investigator. This thing with Sam has been a reality check for me. Sure, it sounds like small-town stuff, but it's scary when you know the police are playing for keeps. I need to put more of a focus on Sam. I need to get ready for the Open. Besides, none of those great leads I had go anywhere."

. . .

I GAVE THREE lessons that afternoon, which put an extra sixty bucks cash in my pocket. Later, I Googled my father on the pro shop computer. The first hit was an article from an obscure golf trade magazine. The title was "Famed British Teaching Pro Lends Name to Driving Range Chain." The story added few details that I didn't already know from Roger, but it had a head shot of my father. I was surprised by the change. His jowls were thicker, his nose pointier, his eyes set closer together. The long sweeping wings of salt-and-pepper hair—the envy of men and women alike—had been hacked into a buzz cut.

KIT NEVER RETURNED to the club, and suddenly it was the day of the hearing and Roger was knocking at the front door. He was in litigation mode—sharp in his eyes, brusque in his manner, moussed in his hair. He looked over the folder of photographs and measurements, muttered a perfunctory thank-you, then closed himself into the den with Sam.

A moment later, or so it seemed despite the passage of an hour, we walked into the stuffy old courtroom that was the Poningo Town Court. I sat in the first row of the gallery while Sam and Roger walked through a wooden gate to one of the counsels' tables. A few people milled around. In the back corner, a clerk shuffled file folders on a desk. On a raised apron below the judge's bench, a court reporter sat on a stool, her knees straddling her steno machine. A court officer parted the heavy velvet drapes, letting in a slab of mote-filled sunlight. They each looked vaguely familiar to me, people I noticed around town in other, less dire contexts. I wondered if they recognized me.

A young man in a dark suit walked down the center aisle carrying a large cardboard box. He bumped through the gate and set the box on the other counsel's table. The words *People v. Chase* were printed on the side in black marker. Roger, I could tell, knew his adversary had arrived but pointedly didn't look over. He continued to sort through his papers, scanning each quickly before setting it down in precise position. Sam sat beside him. I'd never gotten him to the barber, but he looked neat in his tie and blazer and with some creative hairstyling.

The officer announced Judge Henry Chandler, and everyone stood as Chandler swept onto the bench. The Judge stood for a moment, his robes settling around him, and took stock of the courtroom. Everyone sat. The clerk handed him some papers, and as Chandler read them I could see his eyes flicking in Roger's direction. Maybe Roger was right in taking this gambit; maybe he could intimidate Henry Chandler.

"*People versus Chase,*" Judge Chandler muttered as he read. "Samuel Chase. Sam Chase."

I felt myself flush. Chandler looked up from the papers and stared at Sam.

"Well, well. We meet again." Chandler turned to his clerk. "What is this?"

"Felony hearing, Your Honor," said the clerk. "Burglary three."

"The big time, eh?" said the Judge.

He rolled his chair to one side of the bench and called

up both lawyers for a sidebar. I couldn't hear anything other than subvocal grunts, and the meeting quickly broke with a hint of disgust in Chandler.

"Call your first witness," he said.

"The People call Officer Nicholas Cirillo," said the ADA.

The door opened behind me, and I turned to see Cirillo walking down the center aisle. He was dressed in jeans, a button-down Oxford shirt, and a thin sport coat. His badge hung around his neck. Our eyes met solemnly as he passed, like two people acknowledging each other at a funeral.

The clerk swore Cirillo in. Cirillo sat down and settled back in the chair, obviously comfortable with giving testimony in court. The ADA immediately asked what he found when he responded to Harbor Terrace Country Club on the morning in question.

"I was first taken to the locker room, where I saw that a vending machine had been vandalized. The glass front was broken, very little stock remained inside, and there were several torn wrappers on the floor."

"What did you do next?"

"I went outside and determined the likely entry point for whoever vandalized the machine to be an open window in the front of the clubhouse."

The ADA lifted a folder out of the cardboard box. He handed a photograph to Roger, one to Cirillo, and one to Chandler.

"Is that the window you're talking about?" said the ADA.

"Yes," said Cirillo.

"What next?"

"I went inside and determined that the window was located inside the ladies' powder room."

"What did you find there?"

"I picked up a trail of muddy footprints," said Cirillo. "These came out of the powder room, crossed a marble foyer, then crossed a carpeted lobby outside the restaurant to a set of stairs that led down to the locker room."

"Did the footprints reach the locker room?"

"No. They faded about halfway down the stairs."

"Anything remarkable about them?"

"For one thing, there were several sets of them. For another, they all appeared to be smooth-soled rather than treaded."

"And what did that mean to you?" said the ADA.

"It meant they were skateboarding sneakers," said Cirillo.

"Objection!" Roger stood up. "This is a conclusion without any foundation."

Judge Chandler turned to Cirillo.

"What's the basis for your conclusion?" he said.

"I'm the town youth officer. I know these things."

"I'll allow it," said Judge Chandler.

"That's not an adequate foundation," said Roger.

"I said I'll allow it," said Chandler. He stared at Roger, who only slowly sat down.

"What did you do to identify the vandals?" said the ADA.

"The club had been closed the night before," said Cirillo. "I spoke to the restaurant workers, who live in apartments behind the cart barn at the bottom of the hill. They told me a group of teenaged boys often skateboard in the parking lot on nights the club is closed. I used my contacts to identify who those boys may have been. From that point, it was knocking on doors and asking questions. Some boys admitted to being there, others didn't."

The ADA took another photo from his folder and handed copies to Roger, Cirillo, and Judge Chandler.

"Do you recognize that photo?" the ADA said.

"I took it myself," said Cirillo.

"Can you tell me where?"

"Outside the clubhouse below the open window."

"And can you describe it for the record?"

"These are footprints in the flower bed. I placed the ruler beside them for perspective. These prints measured eleven inches from toe to heel."

"And that little square in the center that looks slightly raised?" said the ADA. "What's that?"

"It's a logo."

"Objection," said Roger.

"Overruled," said Judge Chandler.

The ADA handed out another photo.

"What does this show?" he asked.

"It's the same set of footprints taken from a different angle to include the base of the clubhouse wall. It shows the footprints are pointing away from the wall."

"Which means?" said the ADA.

"The person was exiting the clubhouse."

Roger objected, and Judge Chandler overruled. The ADA next pulled two pieces of plaster from the box. He showed them briefly to Roger, then placed them on the rail of the witness box.

"Tell me what these are, Officer," he said.

"These are plaster casts I made of the footprints in the photo," said Cirillo.

The ADA went back to the box and took out a large plastic bag. Inside were sneakers: Sam's sneakers.

"Can you tell me what's in the bag?" said the ADA.

"These are sneakers recovered from the suspect's house yesterday in response to a search warrant."

Prompted by the ADA, Cirillo took one sneaker from the bag and held it up.

"What is that in the center of the sole?"

"It's a square with the embossed letters *JR* in the center."

"And what does that mean to you?"

"It's the logo of a popular skateboarding sneaker."

"Hold the sneaker up against the cast."

Cirillo held up both, then brought them slowly together.

"Do they match?" said the ADA.

"Perfectly," said Cirillo.

"Did any of the footprints inside the clubhouse show that logo?"

"No."

"Can you think of a reason why?"

"None of the prints inside were very clear as to detail."

"But given all the evidence we have seen so far, can you say that the owner of these sneakers was inside the clubhouse that night?"

"I can," said Cirillo.

"How so?"

"You can see from the plaster cast that these footprints

were about two inches deep. They also faced away from the clubhouse wall. The soil was relatively soft, but to create footprints that deep, the person had to be very heavy or had to jump from a height."

"Like the open window?"

"Yes."

"But why not just leave through the front door?" said the ADA.

"All the doors were locked with dead bolts. You needed a key."

"Thank you, Officer," said the ADA. "That's all for now."

The ADA sat. Roger whispered to Sam, then stood up.

"You say you are knowledgeable," said Roger. "Well, Officer, how knowledgeable are you about the popularity of Jake Reed skateboarding sneakers?"

"I know they are very popular," said Cirillo. "The second leading brand."

Roger shuddered. I could tell he was surprised by the answer.

"Yes, well, then wouldn't it be expected that more than one of the boys would have been wearing those sneakers?"

"Yes."

"So how can you say that Sam's sneakers made those footprints?"

"They match," said Cirillo.

"Are there any distinguishing characteristics on the soles of those sneakers, other than the logo?"

"No."

"So you base your comparison on size?"

"Yes."

"What if another boy wore the same sneaker in the same size?"

"It would match," said Cirillo. "Probably."

"Well?" Roger swept back the tails of his suit jacket and set his hands on his hips.

"None of the other boys I spoke to own that sneaker in that size," said Cirillo.

"Move on to something else, Counselor," said Judge Chandler.

"He hasn't proven Sam's sneakers made those footprints," said Roger.

"He doesn't need to prove anything," said Judge Chandler. "This is a felony hearing, not a trial. He just needs to make it appear more likely than not."

"Fine." Roger began to pace behind the table. "How would you describe the softness of the flower bed soil?"

"It was soft," said Cirillo.

"How soft? Like wet sand, like pudding?"

"Firmer."

"Like newly poured cement?"

"That sounds about right."

"How much do you think Sam weighs?"

"A hundred. Maybe one ten."

"Sam weighs one hundred seven pounds," said Roger.

"Objection," said the ADA.

Judge Chandler waved it away.

"How high is the windowsill from ground level?"

"Looked to be about eight feet."

"Very good, Officer. You're a real expert at estimation. It is eight feet five inches." Roger moved around the table and stood right in front of the witness box with his arms folded. "Officer, do you know the formula for calculating the speed of a falling object?"

"Objection," said the ADA.

"Where are you going with this?" said Judge Chandler.

"I want to prove through the laws of physics that someone of Sam's weight jumping from that height into that flower bed would not have made footprints that deep."

"Forget it, Counselor," said Judge Chandler.

"But these are the laws of physics," said Roger.

"And I'm applying the laws of New York," said Judge Chandler. "You are finished with this line of questioning. I'm allowing the plaster casts into evidence."

Roger glared at Judge Chandler, and Judge Chandler glared right back. So much for intimidation.

After a moment, Roger asked to approach the bench. The ADA joined him, and the three men spoke briefly and in whispers.

"I think that's an excellent idea," Chandler said aloud, and pushed himself upright. "In my chambers."

Roger motioned for Sam, and the four of them went through a door behind the bench, followed by the court clerk.

Cirillo let out a long sigh and forced a tight grin. The clerk poked his head back out the door and told Cirillo he could step down from the stand.

"This may be a while," he said.

Cirillo came down the aisle and swung into the row behind me, sitting a little off to the side.

"What are they talking about back there?" I said.

"Settling the case."

"Roger never will settle."

"Yes, he will," said Cirillo. "He strikes me as someone who knows a loser when he sees one."

I leaned forward and rested my chin on the gallery rail, suddenly overcome by what was happening.

"He actually did it," I said. "He was inside. But he said he wasn't."

"Sam's a kid. Kids lie. It's their nature."

"What's going to happen?"

"Exactly, I don't know. Generally, you'll be seeing an awful lot of me for a while."

"Why?"

"Most of my youth officer duties involve counseling kids who have gotten into trouble."

"You're qualified?" I blurted.

"Master's degree."

"Then I apologize," I said. "And I apologize for the way Roger treated you up there. He can be so snide and nasty."

"I don't let a lawyer's courtroom behavior bother me."

"It's not his courtroom behavior," I said. "It's him."

"Then I should offer you my condolences."

"No need," I said. "I have thick skin."

For a moment, I thought I'd set Cirillo up for a predictable locker-room comment. It never came.

"We could make it up to each other by having dinner tonight."

Before I could answer, Roger, the ADA, and Sam came out of Judge Chandler's chambers and took their seats. Roger began sketching on a legal pad in front of Sam.

172

"I think you're right," I said to Cirillo.

"About dinner?"

"About the case settling."

The court officer told everyone to rise. Before I could stand, Cirillo squeezed my shoulder.

"Think about dinner, too," he said.

NINETEEN

WE MET AT Seaside Bobby's, an open-air restaurant above
the town beach that specialized in the finest fried seafood.
The night was one of those rare summer nights that, when
you actually stop to notice, seems all the rarer for its per-
fection. The sky was absolutely cloudless, its color a deep
anil. The water lay like black glass in a curve of gray sand,
with the tiniest gray waves rippling through. In the distance, where the land stretched to a point, a yellow-and-red
Ferris wheel turned against the sky.

"I'm glad you came," Cirillo said after the hostess seated
us. "I wasn't sure you would."

"Neither was I," I said. "You're my son's arresting officer. There must be some rule against this."

"Hypothetically, but not specifically."

"That again?"

"If I'd arrested you, yes. Your son, no. Besides, the case is over."

"I thought the whole point of that deal was that it wasn't over for six months."

The deal was called an adjournment in contemplation of dismissal, or ACD. The case was put on hold for six months with the idea that Sam stay out of trouble. If he did, the case would be dismissed and the file sealed, as if Sam never had climbed through the window and eaten a Snickers bar, which, by the way, he'd finally admitted to me he'd done. One other condition, and what made our rendezvous dicey in the ethical sense, was that Sam was to attend regular counseling sessions with Cirillo.

"It will be over," said Cirillo. "I've handled dozens of kids since I became youth officer, most for doing lots worse than Sam. I've never had one relapse."

"Maybe you missed your calling," I said. "You could hang out a shingle."

"I'm doing exactly what I want to be doing right now."

"Which implies you did something before."

"I taught high school English."

"So that's why . . . ," I said, then thought better of where I was going.

"That's why what?"

"Well, that night you were at my house, when I was on the phone, you were . . ."

"I was looking at your books. Van Doren, Fogel, Burgess. What's a dumb cop doing looking at Shakespearean criticism, right?"

"I never said that."

"No, but you thought it."

The waitress came to take our drink orders. Chardonnay for me, Pinot Grigio for Cirillo. A slight breeze rose, carrying a hint of salt. The tiny waves, silent before, now hissed as they scraped the sand. It was our table that had gone silent.

"So how did you get here from there?" I said. The wine had arrived, and if we didn't turn expansive soon, this night was headed for disaster.

"My father," said Cirillo.

"He was a cop?"

"No, he was a novelist. No one you ever heard of. He was a minor novelist, which I prefer to 'midlist' because it sounds more classical and less corporate. I have some of him in me."

"You want to write?" I said, and thought: Another one, God help us.

"No way. I don't have the patience. My father wrote mysteries. Good versus evil, with good triumphant and very little moral ambiguity. I find the world to be more complicated and more nuanced." He took a sip of wine. "So how does someone go from being an English prof to a golf pro?"

"My father, too," I said. "He was a golf pro in England and brought us, my mother and me, to America when I was very young. I loved those days. He was a pro at a club like Harbor Terrace. I was his shop assistant. We played together every evening after he closed the shop. That's probably not accurate, but that's how I remember it.

"My parents divorced when I was thirteen. My mother

had custody and moved us both away from him, which effectively banished me from golf. But I picked it up again late in high school, played through college, and turned pro after graduation. That's when I met Roger, and it was Roger who ended that career. I fell back on my degree and taught until my own divorce freed me. So here I am, after a seventeen-year hiatus, a pro again and playing in the Open."

"Your father must be very proud," said Cirillo.

"I don't know what he thinks."

Cirillo leaned forward, resting his chin on his hand.

"It was some time in high school," I said. "My mother and I were fighting a lot, and I said something about going back to live with Dad. 'He won't have you,' she said. 'He didn't even contest custody. Just gave you away. He wouldn't have if you were a boy.'"

Cirillo winced. "Was that true?"

"Some things don't need to be true," I said.

The waitress cleared away our plates. Cirillo ordered a port for dessert. I begged off.

"How's your investigation going?" he said.

"I ended it."

He smiled. "I did see you coming out of that house that day, Jenny. I just played along with you."

"You did?"

"There's a certain amount of discretion that goes along with police work. I could have arrested you, but I didn't think you were the breaking-and-entering type."

"Is that why I saw you all over town for the next few days?"

"I wanted to be sure," he said.

"Of what?"

He stared at me. I held his eye a moment, then had to break off. In the distance, the Ferris wheel stopped. I'd taken Sam for a ride on it when he was very young and remembered how the gondolas swayed when the wheel stopped to admit new riders. I felt that way right now.

"Honestly, I didn't know what I was doing," I said. "I had an idea and I ran with it. Right up a tree and out onto a limb. You sawed it off when you told me my prime suspect had an alibi."

"Sorry," he said.

"Don't be," I said. "I wanted to help Kit, but I should have known from the start that I was in over my head. I still need to tell her, and I'm not looking forward to that."

AFTER DINNER, WE took a walk in the park. We bumped hands and a few minutes later held them. A few minutes after that, Cirillo stopped me beside a tree and kissed me. I pulled away.

"I still think this is wrong," I said.

"How?" he said.

I could think of no good reason. My mind was splayed from the wine and the feel of him against me. I kissed him back.

Deep in the park, it was dark. There were bushes, and behind the bushes was a large flat rock, and at the base of the rock the grass was long and soft.

Afterward, we walked hand in hand back to our cars.

"That was my first time al fresco since the B.C. era," I said.

"Before children?"

"No, earlier."

"Before Christ?"

I reared back to smack him.

"No," I said. "I meant Before Couples. Before Roger and I were one."

"Roger," said Cirillo. "I forgot about him."

"So did I."

BACK AT HOME, I swayed in through the front door and locked it behind me. I lifted my keys to the hook and dropped them.

"That you, Mom?" Sam called from the den.

"Yes, it is, honey. I'm home."

A laugh track tittered on the TV. When I stood up from scraping the keys off the floor, I found Sam inspecting me like a drill sergeant.

"What's wrong with you?" he said. "You look all screwed up."

I stepped in front of the hall mirror. I did look somewhat disheveled.

"The ladies and I had dinner. Then we raced back to our cars. I won."

"You're weird," said Sam.

I surreptitiously plucked a piece of grass from behind my ear. So much for the afterglow.

"Kit Gilbert was here," said Sam.

"Here? At our house?"

"That's what I said," said Sam.

"Did she say where she's been all this time?"

"Mom, what are you talking about?"

"Nothing. Sorry." I swallowed hard and got a mental grip on myself. "She's been away the last couple of days. I've been looking for her."

"She said to give you this," said Sam.

He handed me an envelope.

TWENTY

THE NEXT MORNING, I met Kit at the mouth of the maintenance road. I could hear Quint behind the arborvitae, running his skateboard up and down his ramps. Kit didn't look as messy or as frazzled as usual. Her hair was combed neatly, and she wore jeans and a blouse instead of her usual housedress.

"We were at my sister's," she said. "I was looking through the glove compartment when I found it."

"You're sure it's the letter?" I said.

"Definitely. That's the envelope. No stamp, and you can still see the folds. I told you Rick folded it into his windbreaker pocket. Remember?"

I did. I unfolded the letter and read it for the umpteenth time since Sam had handed it to me last night.

NOW I CAN REVEAL WHAT HAPPENED

"Do you have any idea who sent it and what it means?" I said.

"The lawsuit. The little girl dying. It had to be. The timing was right."

I took a deep breath.

"Kit, I've been wanting to talk to you. I was certain the Newmans had a motive to kill Rick. I actually went into their house and snooped for evidence. Almost got caught doing it, too. I found nothing. And it turned out the police looked into it, too. They told me the Newmans were out of town when Rick died. That's important, because if the police believe that, they'll never reopen the investigation."

The corners of Kit's mouth twitched. "But you said—"

"Maybe I shouldn't have said what I said. But I believed it at the time, and now I've found out that I can't push this anymore."

"So you're going to drop me just like that?" she said.

I was about to give her the same line I was giving everyone else lately: that I needed to focus on my life and Sam. I stopped myself. My problems with Sam paled beside her problems with Quint, and golf seemed even more frivolous than usual when set against the life of a penniless widow.

"The only thing I can do is take this note to Detective Donahue," I said. "If anyone can do something with it, he can."

Kit nodded. She wiped the tears from her eyes.

"Guy Amodeo came by this morning," she said. "He told me the club is going to hire him as Rick's replacement. The board has just a few loose ends to tie up. He's going to take over the cottage. He still wants me to stay here. I can't. I've got to get out, Jenny."

"I'll see Detective Donahue this morning," I said. "I promise."

"AM I GONNA be doing this every day?" said Sam.

He slouched deeply in his seat, his feet up on the dashboard.

"Get your feet down," I said. "If we get into an accident and the air bag deploys, it'll break your spine."

"You won't get into an accident."

"Excuse me, I didn't know I was speaking to Nostradamus."

With a deep sigh, Sam pulled his feet off the dash.

"You're not doing this every day forever," I said. "It will be every day for a while, then every other day, then twice a week."

"What's he going to do?"

"Talk to you. Ask you questions about your life, what you want to do, what you hope to do."

"You mean like the kind you ask me?"

"Different ones, I hope. At least from the answers I get."

"It woulda been easier to go to jail."

"Right. You would have loved that," I said. "The good news is you'll get a break when we're at the Open."

Sam didn't react, which gave me the uncomfortable feeling Roger might prevent him from going with me. I decided not to probe. As a child of divorce myself, I was careful, perhaps overly careful, with what I said to Sam.

I stopped in front of a deli that advertised "10¢ photo-copying" and made several copies of the letter and its envelope. I was trying not to get involved in this, trying to disassociate myself from my own curiosity. But I couldn't help being intrigued, especially by the print font. Back in my teaching days, my course syllabus allowed only two fonts: Courier or Times New Roman. I didn't need to be grading papers at midnight and find some wise-ass trying to impress me with twenty-five pages of Gothic print. This font was odd, and I wanted to compare it with the fonts on my word-processing program. When I had a moment.

We parked outside the chain-link pen where the police cars are kept and went inside the building. I wasn't taking part in Sam's first session with Nick Cirillo, youth officer; that much I knew for sure. But I would still encounter Nick Cirillo, suitor, at least for a moment. Would he kiss me (I hoped not) or play it way cool (I hoped not, either) or find some subtle way of revealing the passion that smoldered beneath his workday facade? (Smoldering passion worked for me.) I was never very good at these morning after encounters.

The desk sergeant sent us right downstairs, and I knocked on Nick's door.

"Come in," he called.

I pushed Sam ahead of me.

"Hello, Sam," Nick said heartily. He was in uniform. "Hello, Ms. Chase."

"Hello, Officer," I said.

"Glad you're here on time, Sam. Sorry about the uniform. It doesn't exactly promote open lines of communication, but I'm going out on post when we're done. Sit down." There was only one chair. Nick looked at me. "Thanks, Ms. Chase. We'll be about forty-five minutes."

I backed out of the office and closed the door. Through the pebbled glass, I could see the dark shroud that was Nick's uniform settle behind his desk. Now I wished he *had* kissed me.

But only for a moment, because I had the envelope in my hand and Donahue's office was right down the hall. His door was ajar, and I poked my head in. Donahue looked up from his desk.

"Hi, Jenny," he said. "What brings you here?"

"Sam," I said. "But that's not all. I wanted to thank you for assigning Officer Cirillo to the Rick Gilbert file."

"I didn't," said Donahue. "But he began to ask questions about you, and when he said he suspected you of breaking into a house on Soundview, I thought it was worth giving him a look to see if I missed anything."

"And?"

"I haven't missed anything."

I handed him the envelope.

"Kit brought it to my house last night," I said. "She found it in the glove compartment of her car. It's the letter."

"The letter?" Donahue squinted, momentarily confused. "Ah yes, that letter."

He unfolded the letter from the envelope, read it, then turned it over as if expecting more.

"She's sure this is the letter?" he said.

"It's addressed to Rick and it had no stamp, just as she remembered."

"Why was it in the car?"

"Maybe he was hiding it from her," I said. "I didn't expect you to grill me. This is the first solid thing that at least hints at a threat."

"Sorry, Jenny," he said. "I'm playing devil's advocate, that's all."

"This is it for me," I said. "I told Kit I need to concentrate on my own problems."

Donahue leaned back in his chair. His shoulders relaxed and his eyes softened.

"I heard about Sam. These plea deals often satisfy no one. But I think this was a good result. He'll do well seeing Nick. Kids respond to him. And I'm sorry your career as an investigator is over. I liked our little chats."

I stood and offered my hand. Donahue stood, too, and took it.

"You said finding the letter would change everything," I said.

"Let's hope so," he said. "For Kit's sake."

THE DAY AT the club turned out to be quiet. Few golfers played, which meant few caddies worked, which meant by late afternoon the caddies were acting like idiots. Golf balls whapped against the pro shop awning, pinged across the macadam, and ponged against the cart barn wall in an impromptu game of handball. One caddie climbed the lilac bush and squatted on a branch with his shoulders hunched like a vulture. Three other caddies tied a fourth caddie's wrists to the bag rail, then watched in amazement as the caddie slipped his bonds à la Houdini. Eddie-O yelled. He intercepted the bouncing ball, shook the vulture-caddie down from the lilac, and threatened to tie everyone to the bag rail and leave them till tomorrow.

Charlie and I stayed inside, wincing every time another thud shook the glass door. The disorder outside annoyed me, but as long as Sam wasn't involved, I was staying put. We were in the middle of reconciling the day's receipts with the numbers on the computer/cash register when a huge commotion erupted outside.

"What the hell?" said Charlie.

An electric cart, loaded like a clown car, zoomed past the door. Sam balanced on the front bumper, one hand gripping a roof post and the other pointing forward.

"Goddammit," I said.

"Relax, Jenny. Let Eddie handle it."

The cart circled behind the lilacs, then made another quick pass through the yard. There was a screech, a thud, and a telltale clang of metal. Then silence.

I bolted out from behind the counter.

A circle of caddies ringed the cart, which was nosed up against the barn wall. It was obvious what had happened: The cart had been going too fast for the driver to make the turn into the barn door. Several caddies, still clinging to the back of the cart, cheered and pumped their fists like drunken sailors. But where was Sam?

Visualizing broken bones, I began clawing my way through the circle. The cart hadn't hit the wall directly. Sandwiched in between was a large rubber trash can. Facedown among the dust, grass clippings, and coffee cups was Sam. I hauled him out by a belt loop.

I expected all manner of cuts and bruises, but Sam was as unscathed as the village idiot. He bowed deeply, then extended his arms to the sky and proclaimed, "The Wreck of the Hesperus!"

The caddies cheered wildly. I grabbed Sam by the collar.

"You . . . you . . ." I didn't know whether to smack him in anger or hug him in relief.

He brushed off my hand, then melted away with the rest of the caddies to the other end of the yard.

Eddie-O backed the cart off the trash can, and we both inspected the damage. The can was dented but popped back into shape with a kick. The cart's bumper, a piece of black metal about four feet long, three inches high, and half an inch thick, lay on the macadam. Bumpers on golf carts were more decorative than utile, but I didn't think one should break off so easily.

Eddie-O pushed the two broken bolt stubs out of the holes in the fiberglass body.

"Hey, Jenny, look at these," he said. "Goddamn plastic."

TWENTY-ONE

THERE IS A part of me that demands to act and an equal and opposing part of me that waits to be acted upon. Nowhere is this duality more obvious than in the realm of men. Do I call them, or do I wait for them to call me? I've done both in my life, with varying degrees of tactical success, but my immediate quandary was what to do with Nick. We went out to dinner last night; we had sex under the stars. Yet when I saw him in the morning, he acted distantly official. Or maybe it was officially distant. Not to put too fine a point on it, but what the hell was going on?

My plan was to lie low, which always sounds better in retrospect with the advantage of compressed time than when you are sitting on your porch with a bottle of wine and a pile of AAA TripTiks and tour books to plan your drive to Charleston, West Virginia, and beyond. The beyond part was the kicker. Did I really want to go there right now?

At least Sam wasn't an immediate concern. We were still in the "damn well better not ask" phase of the plea bargain's aftermath, which he apparently decided to negotiate with hours of video games, torpedoes of cola, and bed-pillow-size bags of potato chips. I intentionally refrained from ragging him about issues of health or the unread portion of his summer reading list. He was under my roof for the night, and I needed to cherish the moment.

I poured myself another glass of wine and turned another page of the TripTik. The Lehigh Valley, Gettysburg, the Appalachian Mountains. Sounded great, didn't it?

After a while, my eyes wandered toward the bookcase and the Burgess novel. I was determined not to be sentimental. So what if Nick had looked at these books that night?

By midnight, Sam's video game was silent and a solitary firefly flickered its last in the backyard. I locked up, climbed the stairs, checked on Sam, and tumbled into bed.

I snapped awake at exactly 2:17. Those damn bolts.

I paced my room in the grainy gray darkness, turning everything over in my mind. Was there anything I had forgotten? Was I making any wrong assumptions? No, I decided, and no again.

I went down to the den and pulled the almanac from the bookcase. The sun had risen at 5:18 on the day Rick died. It would rise at 5:35 today. The forecast for this morning was the same: clear and seasonable. Good. I could approximate those basic conditions.

Up in my bedroom, I reset my alarm. Sam wouldn't miss me. He'd still be asleep when I got back. I lay down on the bed, pulled the sheet up to my chin, and tried to still my thumping heart.

THREE HOURS LATER, I sat in my car at the edge of the caddie yard. The sky was bright in the east, but the land itself lay eerily dark, like something out of Magritte. I checked my watch. Two minutes till official sunrise. Across the twelfth fairway, a light popped on in the maintenance barn. One minute to go. I fished the key strap out of my purse, feeling with my thumb for the distinctive nicks on the cart barn key. Something moved in the rearview mirror. I whirled. It was one of the restaurant workers walking up to the clubhouse.

Time came. I got out of the car and closed the door softly behind me. As I crossed the yard, I heard the voices of the greens crew carrying across the empty fairway. Too much activity, I thought. Then I remembered that the crew arrived at a designated time, while Rick always had risen with the sun. There was almost a twenty-minute difference from the day he died.

I lifted the barn door enough to duck inside, then pushed it down behind me. I had fixed that track with a hammer, but the wheel still caught slightly at the kink. From way in the back, a few chargers still buzzed. I looked up. Just as Donahue had said, the air vents in the roof peaks let in outside light. I waited and waited, but my eyes never adjusted to the darkness. The pinpricks of light twinkled like distant, disinterested stars. I couldn't see a damn thing down here on the ground.

Point one, proven.

I flicked the light switch, and two banks of fluorescent lights flashed on. Shading my eyes against the glare, I found the rafter I was looking for. A cart was parked directly below it. I disconnected the charger cable and moved the cart out of the way. A stepladder leaned in the corner. I set it beneath the rafter and climbed up. As I suspected, the top edge of the rafter was splintered, though not in the direction I originally would have thought.

Point two, proven.

I leaned the stepladder back in the corner, rolled the cart below the rafter, and locked the barn. I had much to mull over.

AFTER THE MIDMORNING rush subsided, I dragged Charlie into the barn.

"Cut the lights," I said.

He did. I dragged the door to the ground.

"Geez, Jenny. Has your sexual attraction for me finally overcome you?"

"Shut up, Charlie. What do you see?"

"Nothing."

"Give it a minute."

He gave it about two seconds.

"Still nothing," he said.

"When I found Rick that morning, the lights were off. Donahue told me there would have been enough ambient light for Rick to hang himself with the lights off. I don't think so."

"It's not a sophisticated procedure," said Charlie. "He puts the noose around his neck and jumps."

"Off what?"

"The top of a cart. It's about a five-foot drop."

I flicked the lights back on.

"Think so?" I said.

I lifted the ladder out of the corner and set it up below the rafter.

"You want me to climb that?" said Charlie.

"I want you to look at the rafter and tell me what you see."

Sighing, Charlie climbed the ladder one slow step at a time. When he was high enough, he latched on to the rafter.

"What am I looking for?" he said.

"About a foot to the left of your hand. What do you see?"

"Nothing. A wooden rafter. Wait. I see some splinters on the top edge."

"Good. And knowing what you know about what happened that day . . ." It occurred to me I sounded like Roger. "What do you think caused those splinters?"

"The rope dragging over the edge."

"Which way do you think it would drag the splinters?"

"Down."

"But which way do those splinters point?"

"Up," said Charlie.

"You can come down now."

Charlie stepped onto the ground.

"What are you getting at, Jenny?" he said.

"I'm getting at the possibility that Rick didn't jump off

the top of a cart or anything else. He was hoisted into place and left to hang there."

"That's crazy."

"You saw how dark it was with the lights out," I said. "And you saw the splinters. Now look at one more thing."

I pointed to yesterday's broken bumper, which leaned against the wall below the light switch.

"The bolts holding these bumpers to the cart frames are plastic," I said. "Yesterday, my hundred-seven-pound Sam snapped them off. The rope that hung Rick was tied to a bumper. Don't you think the force of two-hundred-pound Rick stepping off the top of a cart would have snapped that, too?"

"I don't know."

"Well, I do."

"Wait a second, Jenny. Yesterday you were making a case for disengaging yourself from this."

"Yeah, well, I had an epiphany last night."

"So what are you going to do?"

"What I always do," I said. "Call the cops."

I CALLED THE main number and asked for Donahue.

"Who shall I say is calling?" the desk sergeant said. When I told him, he responded with a grunt that suggested I had crossed the imaginary line in his mind from anonymous citizen to local whack-job.

The line went silent, then buzzed internally. The connection clicked.

"Hello, beautiful," said a smooth voice.

"George?"

"No. Nick."

"Nick? I wanted Detective Donahue."

"And good morning to you, too, Jenny."

"Sorry," I said. "Good morning, Nick. The sergeant must have made a mistake. Not that I don't want to talk to you. But I asked for Donahue."

"It's no mistake, Jenny. I'm covering Donahue's calls. He's on vacation."

"You mean he took the day off," I said.

"No. I mean real vacation. Two weeks."

"Two weeks?" I said. I sounded aghast, even to myself.

"Man's entitled to a vacation," said Nick.

"But I saw him just yesterday. He didn't say anything to me."

"Well, I'm sorry, Jen. I don't know what else to say. He's on vacation for two weeks. And it wasn't a sudden decision. We put in for vacation time a year in advance around here."

"Did he tell you anything about the case?"

"What case? Jenny, are you all right? You sound stressed."

"I'm not," I said. "Maybe a little. The Rick Gilbert case. I gave him a letter."

"He didn't say anything to me."

I COULD HAVE saved myself a lot of time by driving a cart across the golf course and gazing down at the harbor from the eighth tee. But I was so hopeful—certain and hopeful—that I drove to the town dock instead. From a distance, the boats were a jumble of indistinguishable masts, riggings, and hulls shimmering beneath the white hot July sky. But as I reached the break in the fence, on the verge of the gang-way descent to the dock, I could see that the *Maggie May* was gone.

I leaned against the fencepost, deflated and confused. Donahue's vacation was none of my business, of course, but his silence when he easily could have told me about it surprised me. Maybe it was because we were both single parents of teenage sons, but I felt more of a connection with Donahue than I felt with Nick. Sure, I'd slept with Nick, but with love often came duplicity. I hadn't yet ruined my trust with Donahue.

"Lose something?"

An old salt sitting on a milk crate in the shade of the clapboard harbormaster's shack looked up from his whittling. His forearms were huge, his forehead tanned and liver-spotted, his eyes a crisp ocean green.

"A person, a boat, my mind." I sounded desperate.

He dug the point of his knife into the wood and scooped out tiny white shards. He was carving a whistle.

"Now which is it?" he said.

"The boat that's usually out at the end there."

I pointed, and he stood up, wood shavings tumbling from his lap. He had a permanent squint to his left eye, and he cocked his head to sight down the length of my arm.

"It's a ketch," I said.

"George Donahue's?" he said. "Gone last night."

"I didn't think it was seaworthy," I said.

"It's not." He sat down and expertly cut a smooth curve along the front of the whistle. "George's been working on that ketch a year, year and a half. I think he finally reached a point beyond his abilities, so he had it hauled out and trucked up to Norwalk. He'll have the experts finish the job."

"So he didn't set sail for Florida," I said.

"Not unless he wanted to die tryin'."

TWENTY-TWO

SOMETHING STRUCK ME as I drove back to the club. I peeled off the circle and parked beside the clubhouse, where tendrils of willows spilled over the stone fence from the adjoining property. Three huge exhaust fans whirred, spewing thick jets of humid, meaty air. A glaze of condensed animal fat coated everything, and my sneakers slipped as I crossed to the Dumpster stockade. The stench of decomposed fruit and rancid meat almost knocked me out. I ducked my head, pinched my hand over my nose, and took as deep a breath as possible before my gag reflex kicked in. The ground here was covered with lemon rinds and lettuce leaves. I skidded quickly to the kitchen door without taking another breath.

Inside, the kitchen was loud and steamy. Two small men in greasy kitchen whites aimed powerful jets of water at huge silver pots. I waved cheerily when they caught sight of me, but they only stared back. Farther in, the air turned stifling. Three large stockpots sat on nests of flame. Steam leaked around their quivering lids.

In a corner, I spotted a man tearing the hearts out of lettuce heads and distributing them into wooden bowls lined up on an aluminum table. I recognized him as the waiter who replaced Reynaldo, which under the circumstances qualified him as an old friend. He worked rhythmically, singing, it seemed, though I could hear nothing above the general din.

I tapped his shoulder. He turned, smiling broadly, and then the smile disappeared as I registered in his mind.

"Reynaldo," I said.

The noise absorbed my voice. He cupped a hand to his ear.

I took a breath and shouted Reynaldo's name. My timing was impeccable, coinciding with one of those strange moments when a cacophony ebbs all at once. Reynaldo's name boomed through the suddenly silent kitchen.

Everyone froze.

From each corner of the kitchen, workers stared at me with expressions that mixed wonder and dread. I looked around, grinning sheepishly at one and all. No one spoke, no one moved.

"Reynaldo," I said. "*¿Dónde fue el?*"

Either they didn't know where he went or didn't care to tell me. One by one, their eyes slid off mine. Sound returned to the kitchen. A cook slapped a hunk of bacon onto a grill, the dishwashers shot water into a bass drum of a pot, the waiter tore into another heart of lettuce. In a moment, I had disappeared.

"YOU MISSED IT," said Charlie. "Investigators from the DA's office raided the maintenance barn. They arrested Guy Amodeo and confiscated a computer."

"Any idea why?" I said. I wondered if *this* was the reason for the odd reaction in the kitchen.

"Some sort of investigation." Charlie smiled his sheepish grin. He knew something. "I made some phone calls. They found porn, possibly child porn."

It's not always a great thing to have your suspicions confirmed. As a parent of a teenager, I often find myself trying to construct solid reality out of shadows. I am told nothing. But I watch and I listen and I try to fit Sam's world together in my mind. Many of my constructs are built on ignorance, fear, and a self-deprecating pessimism. Sometimes I'm right, sometimes I'm crazy. And in my darkest moments with Sam, I prefer crazy to right.

Guy Amodeo's arrest confirmed suspicions I'd felt when I spoke to him in the maintenance barn that day. He had been hiding something from me, and in retrospect the sight of the gooey sandwich wrapper on his lap gave me the creeps. Add his proprietary attitude toward Kit and the cottage, and I wondered whether whatever he was hiding also included Rick.

AT NOON, I crossed the parking lot to the cottage and found both Gilberts on the porch. Quint sat on the top step,

Duke's head pinned in the crook of his arm as he played a handheld video game. Kit sat at the table, flipping idly through a magazine. Behind her stood a wall of cardboard boxes, each box taped and labeled and ready for transport.

I squeezed past Quint, mussing his hair as I stepped onto the porch.

"I gave the letter to Detective Donahue," I said. "Unfortunately, he went on vacation for two weeks."

Kit shrugged. She was dressed just as neatly as the day before—jeans and a blouse again—but a peacefulness had settled into her.

"You heard about the raid?" I said. "Guy Amodeo getting arrested?"

"I did." Kit fought back a curious smile. "I guess he won't be getting the job."

"I doubt he will."

"Which means the club won't throw us out just yet. Was he skimming money?"

"I don't think so. They took his computer."

Kit closed the magazine and pulled at her thumbs.

"That was actually Rick's computer," she said.

"They're looking for porn." I glanced at Quint and lowered my voice. "Possibly kiddie porn. I have no other way to say it than just to say it. I'm beginning to think this is all of a piece. The letter, Guy's arrest, the computer. The same way we thought the lawsuit and the Newmans connected with Rick."

"Until we found out they didn't." Kit opened the magazine and paged through it quickly. "I thought you dropped me."

"I'm back."

"Do you mean that?"

"Yes," I said. "Rick and Guy spent a lot of time together. They were friends. I know this is a reach, but all we can do till Donahue gets back is reach."

Kit closed the magazine again.

"Come with me." She led me down past Quint. "Just as long as we stay in sight, he won't follow."

We stopped at the end of the driveway.

"One day," said Kit, "a long time ago, I was cleaning the bathroom. Quint was not quite a year old, and we hadn't discovered his problems yet. To the side of the toilet was a little wooden door that opened into a crawl space so plumbers could get to the pipes. While I was cleaning, I accidentally knocked the door open. I looked inside and saw this magazine rolled up and jammed into a notch in the pipes. I pulled it out. It had pictures of young kids, you know, naked."

"A porn magazine," I said.

"More like a porn newspaper," said Kit. "It was cheap, and the pictures were blurry. But it was obvious what it was. I showed Rick. He said he didn't know anything about it. Maybe the former greenskeeper left it behind, he said."

"And you believed him?"

"Wanted to believe him. And what he said made sense because we hadn't been in the cottage very long. But I knew better in the back of my mind. And over time things began to dawn on me."

"Like what?" I said.

"Like the way he acted in bed," said Kit. "He didn't

touch me the way he did before. It was more like . . . well, let's just say I spent a lot of time on my knees."

I flashed back to the pictures at the memorial service and how little-girlish—almost little-boyish—the young Kit Gilbert looked.

"We didn't talk about this," Kit continued. "If we didn't talk about money, we sure didn't talk about our sex practices. But Rick did say, and this was after Quint was diagnosed with autism, that we were better off doing what we were doing. We couldn't risk having another child, even a normal one."

"But did Rick have any interest in boys?" I said.

"I never saw anything directly."

"What about indirectly?"

"With everything in my life, you think I needed to imagine anything else?"

THAT EVENING, SAM invited Kieran Boyle over to play video games. Three weeks ago, I would have barred the kid from the house. But such were the ever shifting loyalties and alliances among teens: One day's mortal enemy was, under different circumstances, the next day's best friend. Besides, so much had happened since the missing money incident that Kieran hardly qualified as a malevolent influence in Sam's life. He was a cute kid, now that I was attaching a face to the name for the first time. He was small and small-boned, with long brown smoothly combed hair that fell Veronica Lake style across one eye, the kind of kid, I realized with my changed perspective, men like Rick Gilbert and Guy Amodeo would notice.

I sat at the breakfast counter, writing checks for bills that would come due the week of the Open. Some parents like to muck in with their kids and their kids' friends and try to be pals. I like to hang back, not only to preserve my diminishing authority, but also because I can learn more from listening than from talking.

Most of what they talked about, when they talked at all, was pure adolescent drivel. Amid the fake gunfire and the synthesized screams, they traded information on which friend owned which gaming system and which other friend intended to buy which type of skateboard deck. Then, apropos of nothing, Kieran mentioned the raid.

"The club got a whole lot safer this year," he said.

"Tell me about it," said Sam.

Tell *me* about it, I thought.

"I used to see Guy Amodeo hanging out at the mall a lot," said Kieran. "He was always looking to pick someone up."

Was I hearing this? Did these kids know something it took me three weeks of inexpert detective work and a few strokes of dumb luck to find out?

I barged into the den.

"What are you guys talking about?" I said.

They looked at each other with exaggeratedly ironic expressions, as if I'd imagined their entire conversation.

"I heard you," I said. "You were talking about the raid and then you were talking about Rick and Guy."

They traded quick glances worth many thousands of words. Kieran's asked whether he should continue, and Sam's, to my relief, implied that I was cool.

"They're weird," Kieran ventured.

"I told you that, Mom," said Sam. "Like fifty years ago."

"It didn't mean anything to me then." I focused on Kieran. "How weird?"

"One day I went to the snack bar to buy a soda," said Kieran. "Rick was at the counter, waiting for a burger. I was standing next to him with my hand on the counter so my dollar wouldn't blow away. All of a sudden, Rick put his hand on mine. I like jumped away. And he was like, 'Oh, sorry, I didn't see you.' And I was like, 'Yeah, right.'"

"When did this happen?" I said.

"Last fall," said Kieran.

The doorbell rang.

"And what about Guy Amodeo at the mall?" I said.

"He's there like all the time," said Kieran. "Like mostly in winter."

"What does he do?"

"He sits on a bench and reads a newspaper," said Kieran. "Only he's not reading the newspaper. He's checking people out."

"All people, or just kids?" I said.

"Kids," said Kieran.

The doorbell rang again. I went to the front door. No one was there, and when I stepped onto the stoop for a better look, I noticed an envelope sticking out of the mailbox slot.

I opened the envelope. Inside was a handwritten note: Reynaldo's name, a time, and an address.

TWENTY-THREE

EARLY THE NEXT morning, I taped a page of directions to the dashboard so I could read them on the fly without taking my eyes completely off the road. There was no mystery who left me the note. It had to have been one of the restaurant workers.

The directions took me several miles away from Poningo. The actual address was a vacant lot beside a deli in a seedy corner of an otherwise upscale village. Several dozen men gathered on the sidewalk, almost all of them dressed in baggy jeans and oversize T-shirts with ball caps twisted on their heads. They stood in groups of three or four, hands thrust in pockets, shoulders hunched, eyes glancing furtively at the passing traffic.

I tooled by, searching for Reynaldo. At the end of the street, I made a three-point turn and spotted him on my second pass. I pulled to the curb, lowered my window, and waved. He crossed the street and got into the car.

We drove to a gas station, where I bought two containers of coffee, then parked in a ride-share parking lot near the entrance to a parkway. Reynaldo sipped at his coffee. He looked just as neat and cute as he had waiting tables at the club. But I sensed a distant sadness in him, as if he were in exile.

"I want to talk to you about the morning Rick Gilbert died," I said. "Remember we spoke?"

He nodded.

"I don't know if you know, but I discovered the body. And when you saw me close the barn door, it was so no one else would see him until the cops came."

"I know," he said.

"You didn't pop over to see me by accident," I said. "You saw something, didn't you?"

He nodded again.

"It's important," I said. "Anything you saw."

"I went up to the restaurant early that morning. Before sunup. On way up hill, I hear growling. I see car park near caddie yard and Duke outside it. Like this." He arched his back and dangled his hands, miming a dog on its hind legs. "I keep going up hill, looking back. As I reach top, I see car go into caddie yard and turn into barn."

"It went into the barn?" I said.

"No. It stop at door."

"What did the car look like?"

"Like regular car," said Reynaldo. He traced a contour in the air.

"You mean a sedan?"

"That's it. Sedan."

"What color was it?"

"I couldn't tell. Blue, gray. It was too dark. Not dark like night, but dark. The car didn't have lights on. The door open."

"Which door? Driver's?"

"*Sí.* And when it open, no light come on." Reynaldo tapped the dome light.

"So someone got out?"

"A man. I don't get good look. He go to barn door. Duke run at him. Jumping and jumping. The man crouch. Look like he talk to Duke. That is last I saw."

"What did the man look like?"

"I don't get good look. Short, tall, I don't know. I go to kitchen and pull in bread and stir stockpots. I there about ten minute, then I go back down hill. It was lighter, but still before sunup. I see no car in yard. I get to apartment. As I unlock door, I hear car behind me. I turn. It is car crossing parking lot."

"The same car you saw before?" I said.

"*Sí.* Sedan." He seemed proud to use the word. "It had headlights out. It drove out to road, then headlights came on."

"Which way did it turn?"

"Left."

"Away from town," I muttered. "What else?"

"I go inside apartment. Sleep for little while. Then I get up to go to clubhouse. I don't think of car again until I see caddie yard. It was Tuesday. You usually pull carts onto grass, but I see none. So I walk over and see you."

"Right," I said. "We spoke. Then what?"

"We hear about Rick later in kitchen. We all go outside and watch from top of hill until ambulance drive away. Some go back to kitchen, but I go down hill. I talk to cop, then to detective."

"Donahue?" I said. "A tall man?"

"*Sí*. I tell him what I see. He ask if I see anything else. I say no."

"Did you actually see that car go into the cart barn?"

"No."

"But you think that's what it did."

"*Sí*."

"Then what?"

"Two days later, I wake up early and go up to kitchen. When I come back, there was note on apartment door. It tell me to leave town or I never see my family again."

Reynaldo dug his hand into his front pocket and dragged out a sheet of paper. He unfolded it, then looked it over as if confirming what was written before handing it over.

The note said exactly what he told me. But it wasn't the words that sent the frisson through my body. It was the print font—the same print font as the note to Rick Gilbert.

THE GAS STATION minimart where I'd bought the coffee had a photocopy machine. I made two copies of the note and gave one to Reynaldo.

The sidewalk in front of the vacant lot was empty. I could feel Reynaldo deflate.

"You lost out for the day," I said.

Reynaldo nodded, staring past me.

"What do you get for a day's work?"

"*Cincuenta*," he said. "Fifty."

I scooped my wallet from my purse and assembled $50 from my last stash of lesson money.

"No, no, Miss Jenny," he said.

I pressed the money on him. "Yes, Reynaldo, yes. If I didn't come here, you would be working. It's only fair."

He took the money, gazed thoughtfully at the sidewalk, then shoved the bills into his pocket.

"The ladies miss you," I said. "We all want to see you back at the club."

"Same here," he said.

I drove back to town. Every time I thought of Reynaldo's note, that same frisson coursed through my body. A picture definitely was emerging. It was still vague, still shadowy, still missing many lines that would lend definition to the nebulous shapes. But it promised to resolve into a picture other than the official story of the suicide. If only Donahue weren't on vacation.

I still had some time, so rather than go to the club I headed for the police station. I never made it because I spotted a uniformed Nick Cirillo walking along Poningo Street. I wheeled into a parking space and jumped out of the car. By then, he was half a block away.

"Officer!" I shouted, running to catch up.

Nick turned, smiled, wrapped me in a one-armed em-

brace, and pecked my cheek. We were outside the Garfield
Reading Room. Cindy was in the window, revamping the
summer beach reading display. She winked and rubbed two
fingers shame-shame style.

"I need to talk," I said.

"I'm listening." He patted my butt to start me walking
beside him. "Trouble with Sam?"

I shook my head. "Have you heard from Donahue?"

"No," he said.

"Will you?"

"I don't expect to, but I could. Why?"

"I just made a significant discovery."

Nick was walking the Poningo Street beat, so there were
many interruptions as he poked his head into different shops
or fielded questions from people passing by. We were all the
way at the end of Poningo, on the edge of the village green,
when I finished telling him everything Reynaldo told me.

"This is very interesting, Jen. But there is no mention in
the file that Donahue ever interviewed Raymundo."

"Reynaldo," I said.

"Whatever. And there's no mention of anyone seeing a
car of any description in the vicinity of the caddie yard that
morning."

Across the green, a young mother pushed a stroller to
the base of the library steps and unstrapped her toddler.

"Who are you going to believe, Jenny? Detective Donahue, who has a duty to record every aspect of his investigation, or some restaurant worker who barely speaks
English and probably is here illegally?"

"But isn't that the point?" I said. "Why would an illegal

alien call attention to himself by making up a story like that?"

"You tell me. How well do you know him?"

"He waits our table at the Tuesday luncheons. He tells us about his family, shows us pictures. . . ."

He smiled smugly as my voice trailed off. "What else?" he said.

"Come on, Nick. Cops talk to people every day and make judgments about whether they're telling you the truth or lies."

"We're cops, Jenny. That's our job."

Before I could open my purse and whip out the latest note, a cry came from the library door. That toddler had fallen. Nick rushed over as the mother lifted the baby from the steps. Blood poured from his nose and onto his shirt.

I moved to a park bench. Nick helped the mother wipe the toddler's face and tilted his head back to stop the bleeding. I decided that talking to Nick while he walked the village beat wasn't the best approach. I needed to sit him down somewhere quiet and make my case. I stood up, caught his attention, and waved that I was leaving.

"Remember Sam's appointment," he called after me. "Two o'clock."

EXTRAPOLATING THEORY FROM my own experience, I believed that if you spent lots of time with a person with a strong personality, you tended to adopt that person's manner of thinking and became skeptical of your own. If you are a woman and that strong personality is a man, the skepticism runs even deeper. I had the fortune, or misfortune, of having two strong male personalities in my life. When I expressed an opinion about anything, they immediately beat it into the ground.

My professional life was much different, whether it was golf or academia. My opinions and talents were validated, cultivated, sometimes even cherished. I wrote and defended a thesis. I published articles in obscure intellectual journals. I even had a short story accepted by a literary magazine, though the magazine, alas, went out of business before my story appeared in print. And in a few days, I was playing in the U.S. Open. Take that, Dad. Take that, Roger.

Years removed from my father, and years removed from my marriage, I was less patient with men who treated me like a little girl. Charlie treated me with respect. He had to. Not only did he harbor dreams, he also knew I could irretrievably screw up his pro shop with a few clicks of a mouse. So did Eric Garfield. Whenever he threw a party, he always managed to corner me to elicit my "professional opinion" on this book or that.

Now came the cops. Donahue was "old school" but polite enough to bite back his amusement and, I believed, open-minded enough to look into my crazy clues. I expected even more from Nick. He was younger, which I suppose made him "new school," and he had an academic background. Plus we had whatever it was we had between us. I hoped he wouldn't doubt me.

I passed the Reading Room and found myself in front of the Autism Awareness Center. The AAC occupied half of what had been a Woolworth's in simpler times. The big front windows remained, and in the AAC's portion framed poems written by autistic children were on display. I read one and then another, feeling my agitation settle and my anger at Nick dissipate. The old reliable. Put a text in front of me and I couldn't not read it, couldn't not become engaged.

The poems were not good on any absolute scale. They were full of trite images, unscanned lines, and unschemed rhymes. But considering the authors, wow, they were terrific. And then the last poem stopped me cold.

First off, it was the best of the poems by far. It was composed of three stanzas, each one describing a beach. The first two stanzas were playful and innocent, the third brooding and dark. But the surprising turn of emotion in the last stanza wasn't what chilled me.

Fumbling, I got the two notes out of my handbag.

The poem was printed in the same font.

I SWUNG BY the house to pick up Sam. It was ten o'clock, too late for him to make a loop and keep his two o'clock appointment at the police station. But I preferred him idling in the caddie yard than idling alone at home.

At noon, I walked over to the cottage. As I waited for Kit to answer my knock, I heard strange sounds coming from the top of the stairs.

"Quint," Kit said as she let me in. "He's taking a bath. He doesn't take them often, but when he does they last for hours. That's what he calls his bubble talk."

We went into the living room. Several open and empty boxes nested in a corner, and I could see that books and knickknacks now stood on shelves that had been bare a few days before.

"The board told me they won't be able to hire anyone soon," she said. "So why not unpack."

"That's good."

"Not good, but it's at least less bad. I'll take that for now." She sat on the couch and waved me toward a chair set kitty-corner. "Maybe you're here to tell me something good."

"Sorry, no." I sat. "But I have a question. You once said something about a play group with other boys like Quint."

"You can say autistic, Jenny. It's not a bad word."

"Right. Well, you said something about a play group with these autistic kids. How many were there?"

"About five or six," said Kit. "There were more kids involved, but it was rare when all of them showed up at the same time."

"Do you remember names?"

"Did you find something?"

"No," I said. "I'm trying to get as big a picture as I can, in case Donahue asks me questions when he gets back."

"He'll be back soon?"

"I hope so. But it is a two-week vacation he's on." And meanwhile I had this little thing called the U.S. Open. "Did Quint ever go to the AAC?"

"Once." Kit frowned. "They asked us not to come back. He was too aggressive with the other kids, too rough with the computers. They're very big on computers there."

"So I've heard," I said.

"And the funny thing is, he plays video games here and he's always so careful and gentle. His Game Boy is three years old and it looks like it just came out of the box."

"Do any of the play group boys go to the AAC?"

"I'm sure they do," said Kit. "But the names. That was years ago. And some things you think you'll never forget, well, sometimes you do. Would names help?"

I half nodded, half shrugged. What the hell did I know?

"We took some pictures. They're packed away somewhere. I'll dig around. Maybe looking at them will jog my memory."

TWENTY-FOUR

A MIDWEEK, MIDAFTERNOON in July, and the AAC was quiet. A few adolescent boys slouched in front of laptops in the computer lab. Some played games, others pecked randomly at the keyboards. A frail boy with a big head of reddish hair stared at a swirl of galaxies fading and reappearing on his computer screen.

"He's one of our best writers," whispered the assistant director, a neat, high-strung woman who'd buttonholed me as soon as I walked in the door. The nametag on her lapel said "Chris Gauman."

We watched the boy watching his screen for almost a minute, as if waiting for something significant to happen. The central air kicked on with a faint *whoosh*, and a cold, faintly musty draft settled around me.

Ms. Gauman ushered me away from the lab and into the main lounge. It was designed with nonthreatening earth tones and furnished with plumply upholstered sofas and chairs. We sat in two corner chairs, a table piled with well-thumbed magazines in between. The seat cushion was so soft, I needed to perch myself on the front edge to keep from being swallowed.

"Our writing program wasn't meant to be our main focus," said Ms. Gauman. "But a corporation donated the laptops, so we needed to find some way to use them. One of the parent volunteers suggested a writing lab as a means of getting these children to express their feelings in positive ways."

"Poetry lends itself to that," I said.

Ms. Gauman cocked her head as if confused.

"What I mean is that a poem can be as simple as a series of discreet images, rather than a lengthy narrative."

"That's correct," she said, realizing that we were in agreement. "Although we have some children with the ability to write coherent narratives. Where is it you teach again?"

"Manhattanville. My concentration is modern American and British literature."

"Then you read the book about the autistic boy and the dead dog."

"The week it came out," I said. "Great book."

"Yes, he really captured the essence of the autistic mind," said Ms. Gauman. "But I'm still not quite clear on why you're here."

"My department head requires every professor to propose one new course per academic year." I cupped a hand beside my mouth as if letting her in on a big secret. "I mean, really. What possible angle in English hasn't been done to death a hundred times?"

"I wouldn't know," she said. "I was a sociology major."

"Trust me, there isn't," I said. "Anyway, I was passing by last night and saw the poems in the front window. I read them, and all of a sudden it hit me. I could offer a course called 'The Poetry of Autism.'"

"Interesting," she said.

"I saw it as an interdisciplinary course," I said, "taught with a psychology professor."

Ms. Gauman grunted politely. But I could see a glaze rolling across her eyes and a furtive glance at her wristwatch.

"I called a friend in the Psychology Department and got her on board. Now I need to write a proposal, and to write the proposal I need sample poems written by autistic children."

Ms. Gauman blinked. I had her full attention now.

"How many would you need?" she said.

From where I sat, I could see the poems hanging in the front window. There were six.

"About six," I said.

"What is your time frame?"

"It would be for the spring semester. The deadline for the proposal is September first."

"That's good," said Ms. Gauman. "We'll have some time to put your request through the proper channels."

"What channels?"

"Before anything written by any of our children can be

used outside the context of the AAC, the child's parents must sign a release."

I must have appeared incredulous.

"We can't have people profiting from our children's therapeutic endeavors," she added.

"Who's profiting? I'm proposing a course I may never teach."

"You get paid, don't you?"

"Yes, but I hardly call that profiting."

"Well, I'm sorry."

"What about those?" I pointed at the front window. "They're already in the public domain."

"Sorry," she said. "Rules are rules."

"How long would it take to get the releases?"

"You need to make a written request to our director. She will contact the parents for the releases. It's summer. Things like this always take longer in the summer with people on vacation."

"How about the ones in the window?" I said. "Could you give me those people's names and let me contact them directly for the releases? I promise not to use the poems in the proposal unless I get them."

"I can't tell you the names," said Ms. Gauman. "That in itself would be a breach of confidentiality."

CIRILLO WAS PARTIALLY out of uniform when I dropped Sam off for his two o'clock session. The white uniform shirt was gone, replaced by a stiffly starched powder blue bowling shirt with "Nick" stitched onto the pocket. His hair was wet and spiky, as if he'd just soaked his head in a sink.

"I need to talk," I said as Sam squeezed past and took a seat in Cirillo's office.

"I'm all ears," said Cirillo. His tone sounded conciliatory.

"Not now. It'll take too long," I said. "How about tonight? Dinner?"

"Seaside Bobby's?" He grinned suggestively.

"My house," I said. "Seven-thirty."

"I'm there."

He closed the door. I watched his watery image move behind the pebbled glass.

"Hey, Sam," his voice boomed heartily. "How they hanging?"

I walked down the corridor. Donahue's office was dark and quiet. I rattled the doorknob, then stood with my eyes closed, trying to divine when he would return.

"WHY CAN'T I?" said Sam.

His voice had deepened over the last few months but still could sound the whiny tone he'd inherited from Roger.

"Because," I said.

"You already said that."

We were in my bedroom. A large suitcase yawned on my bed, half-filled with golf outfits. The pungent aroma of bell peppers simmering in olive oil and garlic permeated the entire house.

Sam's request was simple. All the boys were going to skateboard that evening. I had no reason to deny him, other than the simple fact that he hadn't been out of the house at night since the hearing.

"You can go," I said. "But with the same rules we had

before. Plus you call me if you go anywhere else, and I don't mean after you get there."

"Yes, Mom, I will." He bolted into the hallway.

"Come back here," I said. He did, leaning against the doorjamb. "You need to pack."

"Do I?"

"Yes, you do. Ten days of clothes."

"Ten days? The Open's like less than a week."

"Ten days. And don't forget socks and underwear."

Sam went into his room. Drawers squeaked open and slammed shut. Hangers rattled in the closet. I checked my watch: almost time to prepare the chicken. I began to zip up the suitcase, then stopped. I didn't want to make things too easy for Nick.

I went down to the kitchen. A minute later, Sam zoomed through.

"All packed," he said.

He grabbed his skateboard from the porch.

"Aren't you going to eat?" I called after him.

"Already did," he yelled back.

I went to the den window just in time to catch a glimpse of him rolling down the street. I felt guilty, parenting-wise, for giving in against my better judgment and for my own convenience. But I couldn't expect to keep him locked up in the house for six months.

Nick showed up ten minutes later. He wore faded jeans and a yellow polo shirt and had studiously cultivated jawline stubble, perhaps from shaving at bedtime rather than morning. He kissed me hello and presented me with two bottles of wine, a warm Merlot and a chilled Sauvignon Blanc.

"Best I could do without knowing the menu," he said.

We went into the kitchen. He opened the Blanc while I ladled the sauteed peppers onto the tray of marinated chicken. A bell chimed, the oven hitting 350 degrees. I opened the oven door and pushed the tray inside. When I backed away, Nick's arms wrapped me from behind.

I spun. We kissed. I could taste the spearmint on his tongue. I also could sense that he was treating dinner as a date with incidental discussion while I planned a discussion wrapped within a date. I patted his chest, and he loosened up.

"We have half an hour," I said. "Let's sit."

He followed me to the porch and settled on the wicker love seat while I poured us each a glass of wine. He hadn't left me much room, so I folded myself tight and, sitting sideways, wedged my feet under his thigh.

"I found out who killed Rick Gilbert," I said.

"You did?" he said. "Who?"

"I don't have a name yet. But I know where to find it."

"But aren't you presupposing someone killed him when there is no evidence of murder?"

He spoke lightly, as if struggling to indulge me rather than just shut down the conversation. He put a hand on my knee and slipped it down (really up) my thigh. I blocked the advance with my elbow.

"Oh, there's evidence," I said. "First, I wondered if a five-foot drop from the roof of a golf cart was enough to kill a man Rick's size."

"It must have been because it did," said Nick.

"Then I got to thinking that he looked almost too clean.

No piss on the floor, no shit in his pants, no erection. His neck barely looked broken."

"It wasn't," said Nick. "But it didn't need to be. He died of asphyxiation. A compressed windpipe."

He tried the knee again, kneading it with his thumb.

"Well, something happened at the club that got me thinking."

"You seem to be doing a lot of thinking."

"That's what I do," I said. "Sorry."

I told him about the plastic bumper bolts and how I didn't think they could withstand the force of Rick Gilbert hanging himself and how I had inspected the rafters in the cart barn. He listened. I'll give him that much.

"Very sophisticated," he said when I finished. He leaned close and kissed me. I tolerated the kiss for several seconds but broke it off when I felt his fingers hook my belt.

"Jenny," he whispered.

"Nick," I said aloud.

The phone rang. I unwedged my feet and got up, but he tugged me back down.

"I need to answer that," I said. "It's Sam checking in."

"Okay," he said. He trailed a hand up the back of my thigh and pinched my butt. "Hold that thought."

I went into the kitchen and answered the phone.

"I'm still at Willy's, Ma," said Sam. "But we're going over to Brian's. He has a new jump he built."

"That's fine. Are you going to stay at Brian's?"

"Oh yeah. If we go anywhere else, I'll call."

"Very good, Sam. Thanks for calling."

I gently hung up the phone and peeked into the porch

as Nick rose off the love seat and topped off my glass of wine. This wasn't going the way I'd expected. Maybe my expectations were too high or simply on a different plane.

I went back to the porch. Nick was stretched out comfortably on the love seat. He patted the sliver of cushion beside him.

I swung a chair out from the table and sat down.

"Let's go back to square one," I said.

"With us?" he said.

"With Rick Gilbert."

"I get the feeling there's always some third party around." He looked behind the love seat. "If it isn't Sam, it's Rick Gilbert; if it isn't Rick Gilbert, it's Donahue."

"Square one is Donahue telling me that to reopen the investigation, he needed evidence suggesting an alternate theory." I proceeded to lecture Nick point by point. First there was the anonymous note stuck in Rick's mailbox. I slipped the copy from the folder on the table and laid it on Nick's lap. Next there was my meeting with Reynaldo. (I skipped over my detour into the Newman residence.) I conceded that Nick had already told me there was no reference to Reynaldo in Donahue's case notes. But remember what he told me, I said, and now look at this.

I handed Nick the copy of the note Reynaldo found on his door.

"So someone wanted him to get out of town?" he said. "You already told me this."

"Look at both notes."

He held them side by side, his face screwed up in doubt, confusion, and severely diminishing patience.

"Same font," I said. "It's called Sydnie. You don't see it very often. And believe me, I used to see a lot of print fonts."

"So it's an obscure font. What does that prove?"

"I don't know yet. But what are the chances that two different people would send anonymous notes to Rick Gilbert and Reynaldo in the same font?"

"I don't know," Nick said wearily.

"There's one more thing," I said.

I expected a retort along the lines of "I can hardly wait" but didn't get it. I stood up and held out my hand. He gave me back the two notes. I put them on the table and held out my hand again. This time he took it and pulled me onto his lap.

"Let's forget about Rick Gilbert," he said. He kissed me all around the mouth, quick pecks that sent a not unpleasant chill running up and down my spine.

"I can't," I said, squirming. "Not until I show you what else I found."

He stopped kissing and pressed my cheeks.

"You're serious about this," he said.

I nodded between his hands.

"Okay, show me."

"We need to go into town," I said. "That's where it is."

"What about dinner?"

"The chicken still needs about twenty minutes. We'll be back easily."

We took my car and said little on the way. I sensed a distance in Nick—he clung to the ceiling handle over the passenger door and rested his chin in the crook of his elbow—but I wasn't sure whether it was personal or professional or he simply wanted to get this over with.

Poningo Street was empty after business hours. I pulled to the curb right in front of the AAC. I gave no hint, just steered Nick directly to the poem. He stared at it long enough to have read it, glanced at me, then read it again, this time stroking his chin.

"Not bad," he said. "Not just for one of those kids, but for anyone."

"Don't you notice anything else?" I gave him a moment, then pulled the two notes from my pocket and held them up to the window. "The same font."

"I have to give you that one," he said. "But what does it mean?"

"The Gilbert boy, Quint, is autistic. Several years ago, his mother organized a play group with other autistic boys. It didn't last very long. The boys functioned at different levels, and that's what eventually pulled it apart. Some of those boys, the higher-functioning ones, come to the AAC.

"I've talked to Kit about Rick. Very personal talks. And with what she told me, let's just say that Rick had a somewhat ambiguous sexuality." I let that sit a beat. "Kit found kiddie porn in the house."

"Jesus," said Nick.

"You know what happened at the club the other day. Rick and Guy Amodeo were close. But you add kiddie porn and access to mentally challenged, prepubescent boys, and you've got something."

"What?" Nick looked at his watch. I didn't need to be

told we were cutting the twenty minutes close, but I didn't care.

"I came here this afternoon and pretended I was writing a proposal for a course on autistic writing. The assistant director was very polite and very interested, until I asked for some writing samples. She couldn't give me any without a release, and the process for getting a release would take days, maybe weeks."

"Can't you just copy them?" he said mildly.

"Are you even listening to me?" I said. "I don't want the poems. I want to know who wrote this one to see if he was in that play group."

"So get the release. Donahue won't be back for several days."

"It'll take longer than several days. Maybe several weeks. I was thinking you could get a warrant to find out who wrote that poem."

"Based on what?"

"The anonymous notes and this." I rapped my knuckles on the glass.

Nick laughed. "You want me to get a warrant based on a font?"

"You got a warrant for Sam's sneakers based on a logo and a footprint."

"I didn't get that warrant. The DA's office did."

"You were there."

"As a courtesy to protect you."

"Some courtesy. Next time, don't feel a need to be so polite."

"Jesus, Jen." He took a deep breath, grappling with the need to speak rationally. "The situation with Sam was different. We knew he had been at the club that night. We had the same footprints inside and outside the clubhouse."

"And I have these." I waved the two notes.

"It's different," said Nick.

"The only difference I see is that it's you who believed Sam broke into the clubhouse while it's I who believe someone killed Rick Gilbert."

"Well, yeah."

"So you're right and I'm wrong, even though the sequence of my thought processes is just as logical as yours. Maybe more."

"I think you're trying to abuse my position," he said.

"No, Nick, I think you're trying to abuse mine."

TWENTY-FIVE

IT WAS TIME to second-guess myself.

Maybe I came across as too hard and too strident.

Maybe I should have chosen a menu without the prep time that allowed us to drive to the AAC.

Maybe I should have been more patient and served dinner first. Plied with food and wine, Nick might have been more cooperative. I could have gotten what I wanted, and he could have gotten what he wanted. Instead, I'd rubbed away the social conventions of what would have been a successful, productive, and, dare I say, romantic evening.

I finished cleaning the kitchen and packing away the chicken in Tupperware. This was normally the juncture where I would phone Cindy and invite her over and blubber about how I blew another one. But I didn't feel like calling Cindy tonight. I needed to get through this one on my own.

The last of the Sauvignon Blanc stood on the porch table and had gone warm in the evening air. Truth be told, the finish tasted like grapefruit juice. I corked it and poured myself a Chardonnay. Then I noticed the clock. It was nine-fifteen, and I hadn't heard from Sam.

I went into the hallway and dug my cell phone from the basket where I'd tossed it after Nick and I parted ways on the front lawn. No voice mail messages; no missed calls. I went up to my bedroom, sat on the bed, and checked the caller ID. This was the move that had started it all, the loose end I had tugged to send the whole ball of my life rolling across the floor, unraveling as it went. Without ticking through the call log that night, I don't see Rick Gilbert's calls, don't get involved with Kit, don't start investigating Rick's death, and maybe keep a close enough eye on Sam that he's not involved in the clubhouse break-in. But I did look at my call logs that night, and I did it because of my father. Like it or not, your monumental decisions go back to the important influences in your life.

The last logged call was Sam's telling me the boys were going to Brian's house.

I went back downstairs and paced the porch. He was only fifteen minutes late in calling me, I told myself. That didn't necessarily mean anything other than that he forgot. But I couldn't separate Sam from my own disaster of a night with Nick. ("What the hell was I thinking?" Nick had said before driving away.)

I opened my cell phone and speed-dialed Sam's cell number. His phone rang, then kicked into voice mail.

"Sam, this is your mother. It's nine-eighteen, and I haven't heard from you."

Usually, Sam called back right away. He always had some excuse, like he couldn't get the phone out of his pocket in time or he was just about to call. But one long minute dragged by and then another. At nine-twenty, I called him again. The phone kicked into voice mail again. I didn't leave a message. Instead, I broke the connection and redialed. I did this seven or eight times in rapid succession, all the while pacing the porch like an insane woman. I didn't care. I was livid at Sam for ignoring me, which presupposed he knew I was calling him. The more logical explanation was that the boys had taken their cell phones out of their pockets while they performed tricks on Brian's new jump and that Sam's phone, always set on vibrate, buzzed like a dying cicada on the top of a stone wall.

I went to the phone book and pawed through the pages. Calling a family's land line in search of an errant child was an extreme move in these times. It smacked of loosened familial bonds, or at least unpaid cell phone bills.

I composed myself and called anyway.

"They left about a half hour ago," Brian's father said.

"Did they say where?"

He gave me another boy's name. I thanked him, hung up, and went back to the phone book. No stopping me now; I was hot.

The mother answered at the next boy's house. I knew none of these parents, mind you, though I'd probably seen them at school functions.

"Yes, they're outside," she said. "Do you want to talk to him?"

"Please," I said. "That would be grand."

She put down the phone with a clunk. I heard her opening a door, shouting Sam's name. My worry gave way to relief, then shaded back toward anger. The phone lifted.

"Sam," I growled.

"No," said the woman. "I thought they were outside, but they're gone. The rascals didn't tell me where."

I grabbed my car keys. Chasing around town and looking for Sam was the act of an irrational mind. On the driveway, I made one more stab at rational thought. It was nine twenty-five, I told myself. He hadn't left town, hadn't broken into someone's house, hadn't been kidnapped. He simply hadn't called at the appropriate time. There were reasons, probably logical and probably benign.

I took a deep breath, catching a whiff of the honeysuckle that grew in a thick mat over the neighbor's wooden fence. From a distance came the drone of skateboard wheels on pavement. See, I told myself, he's on his way home. But almost immediately the sound resolved into a semitrailer downshifting to exit the interstate. I looked at the cell phone. Nine-thirty changed to nine thirty-one, and another pang of anxiety stabbed me.

"Call," I pleaded.

I got into the car and backed out of the driveway. As I drove past Cindy's house, the cell phone rang. I snatched it up, my trust in my son immediately restored, all unconditionally forgiven. But the little window showed the caller wasn't Sam. It was Nick. I tossed the phone onto the passenger seat and strangled the steering wheel with my fingers.

Sam often spoke about the places he skateboarded, and I must confess to ignoring the details because I didn't want to dignify his skateboarding when I wanted him to be playing golf. He had mentioned a set of concrete steps. Where? I didn't know. He had mentioned a steep hill. Where? You got me again on that one. But I knew that a neighborhood across town recently had its roads repaved after an endless sewer project. It was hilly, too, perfect for skateboarding.

Sure enough, I found several knots of kids walking and skateboarding around the streets. I slowed down and eyed them carefully. None of them was Sam.

I pulled over and looked at the phone. It was nine thirty-five. I tried Sam but cut the call after the second ring. Then I remembered one place he possibly could be.

The town skate park was relatively new, built in the playground of a disused elementary school that was converted into office space for school district administrators. It was nothing like the abstract moonscapes Sam once showed me in a magazine, but a collection of ramps, half-pipes, and grinding bars bolted to the pavement in seemingly random fashion.

"It sucks," Sam had said after his first visit, but that obviously was teenage posturing. He'd gone back many times since.

I sensed something wrong the moment I stepped out of the car. The park was crowded, but no one was skating. All the kids were gathered on a large ramp in one corner of the park. They held their boards under their arms or leaned them against their hips and were seemingly transfixed by something happening in the opposite corner of the park. I couldn't see what they were looking at. A line of shrubs planted alongside the park's chain-link fence blocked my view.

Something else was different, and it took me a moment to realize exactly what. The park was floodlit, as usual, the lighting so powerful that it bleached the color out of everything inside. But the music that usually blared over the loudspeakers was silent. Instead, a guttural moan floated through the night air.

I reached the outer ring of adults. A couple of shaggy-haired park employees stood at the gate, letting no one in or out.

"What happened?" I said.

"He went crazy," said the man next to me. "Started whaling at kids with his board."

I spotted a boy sitting on the ground with his back against the gatehouse. A park employee pressed a white cloth against a bloody gash on the boy's forehead. A second boy lay beside him, holding a bandage to his chin. A wobble shook my knees, but I fought it off as I scanned the crowded ramp. Sam was there. Unbloodied, skateboard in hand.

I felt instantly relieved, instantly grateful. Sam was neither the *he* nor one of his victims. Plus, there was no way he could have called during this.

"Who is he?" I asked.

"Don't know," said the man. "He climbed up one of the basketball poles. Father's trying to talk him down."

The basketball goals—there were two, one at each end of the skate park—were relics from the parking lot's days as a school playground. Each goal was supported by two metal poles sunk into the ground and held together by metal clamps at three-foot intervals. At the top, more than ten feet up, four struts flared out and attached to the backboard. The bottom six feet of each pole was wrapped with padded canvas.

I couldn't see anything from where I stood. The farther goal was empty, while the shrubs blocked my view of the ground and an overhanging tree blocked my view of the closer one. I circled behind the adults. The basket came into view first. The boy stood behind the backboard, his legs locked on the top two struts.

"Danny, hand me the board and come down." It was an adult voice, smooth, calm. And familiar.

The boy swung his skateboard sharply, as if batting away an insect or warding off an attack. After a moment, he swung again, and the momentum of the follow-through almost pulled him off the basket. The adults around me gasped.

"Danny, you'll hurt yourself."

Danny looked down. He was a stocky boy with a round face and slick brown hair. He was dressed like all the other boys in an oversize T-shirt and long baggy shorts. There were bloodstains on the shirt. Danny adjusted himself so that he stood with both feet on one of the two lower struts. He almost lost his balance but caught himself. Another gasp rose from the adults.

"That's it, Danny. Easy now," came the voice.

Danny's face was puffy and flushed from crying. He leaned forward as far as he could and dangled the skateboard by its wheels.

"Okay, Danny, drop it."

The boy let go of the skateboard.

I began knifing through the crowd for the nearest point along the fence where I could see past the shrubs. The boy swung his legs again and sat on the strut, looking down.

"Whenever you're ready, son. You tell me when."

I was just at the fence when Danny pushed off the strut. I saw his father catch him and roll to the ground to absorb the shock. By then, I already knew whom I would see.

"WHO WAS THAT boy on the basketball hoop?" I said.

Sam had been scared. I had seen it in his eyes when the incident finally ended and the skate park workers let the kids who had been on the ramp go out through a side gate, counting them as they passed. He looked small in the front seat, his skateboard covering his chest like a Roman shield. Bands of street light licked across him as we tooled down Poningo Street. I was in no rush. Once we got home, he'd go directly to the computer or his video games or his MP3 player, and I'd fade to a shadow at the edge of his consciousness.

"His name is Danny. He comes to the skate park about once a week."

"Does he come with friends or alone?" I said.

"He hangs out by himself."

"Is his last name Donahue?"

"Yeah, I think so."

"You saw the man who got him down. That was Detective Donahue. Remember him visiting our house?"

"Yeah."

"So he's Danny's father?"

"Well, duh, Mom. They have the same last name."

At another time, I would have lectured him about how facts that seem so self-evident as to merit a "duh" from a teenage genius aren't always so obvious to those older and more experienced at being wrong in our assumptions. Besides, Sam was looking more comfortable by now. He let the skateboard slip to the floor, and his chest pushed against the seat belt. He was regaining his bravado, courtesy of me.

"Do you know Danny Donahue?" I said.

"I see him in school."

"He lives in Poningo?"

"Port Byram. He's in special ed classes with some other weird kids. They're all from out of town."

"What kind of weird?" I said. With Sam, the possibilities were boundless.

"I don't know," said Sam. "He's weird like Quint Gilbert is weird. Only not as weird."

"What happened tonight?"

"I don't know. I didn't see it."

Sam never saw anything.

"Come on, Sam. Even if you didn't see it, you must have heard something from someone who did. You were stuck on that ramp for twenty minutes that I saw."

"Danny was in a corner doing Ollies, and a couple of kids made fun of how he did them. He stared at them and they stared back and the next thing Danny started whacking them with his board."

"Was his father there?"

"No," said Sam. "The guy in the booth called the cops. They came pretty fast, but by then Danny was already up on the basket. Then his father came. He told the cops to leave. You saw the rest."

TWENTY-SIX

"IT'S NOT TOO late," Kit said for the second time.

The first was when she answered the door and I apologized for the hour. Now, standing in the living room, she touched a finger to her lips and pointed up. Above us, creaking footfalls rolled across the ceiling.

"He's having one of his nights," she said. "Pacing nights, I call them."

"How long?"

"Till he collapses. If I'm lucky, he'll collapse on the bed. Then all I'll need is to tuck him in."

She untied her belt, pulled her bathrobe tightly across herself, and redid the knot.

"Sit," she said, and we did. "What time is it, anyway?"

"Almost ten-thirty."

Kit lifted her eyes to the ceiling as Quint made another pass.

"Wow," she said, which could have meant Quint either just had started pacing or had been pacing for a long time.

"I was wondering if you found anything about the play group," I said.

"I did." Kit patted her pockets, then leaned sideways to look over the arm of the sofa. "Here."

She dragged out a shoebox brimming with photos. A few rode on top, clipped together. She dealt these onto the cushion beside her.

"This is the one with everybody."

She handed it to me.

The photo was taken on the front steps of the cottage. It was a cloudy day, with a pervading sense of gray bleakness even though you couldn't see the sky. There were seven women—seven mothers, I assumed, despite my undelivered lecture to Sam—and seven boys. The mothers were sitting, while the boys, who looked to be about five or six years old, stood between their knees. I picked out Kit and Quint. They were on the right side of the group, set a little apart. Symbolic, I wondered, or just happenstance?

"Rick took the picture," said Kit. "That's why everybody was in it. It was mid-March, the ugliest time of year at a golf course because everything's muddy and the grass hasn't started to grow. Rick would come home for lunch with his boots caked with mud. I wouldn't let him into the house, which is why this picture was taken outside. Funny how I'm clear on that, but fuzzy with the names." She tapped the side of her head. "It's all in here, like files in a computer, but then you try to access them and you can't."

"Frustrating," I said. "I find that happening more and more every day."

I got up from the chair and held the photo under the lamplight at the closest distance possible without it going out of focus. The seven boys all were bundled in jackets or sweatshirts. One had a hood over his head and the cords pulled so tight that only his nose and eyes showed. Another boy, standing in the lower left corner, looked to be more heavyset than the others. Like a harbor seal.

"Do you remember this boy?" I pressed a thumbnail beside the boy's face, blocking off everyone else in the picture.

Kit scooted closer. "I think it's . . . No, sorry."

"Could his name have been Danny?"

"Could have been Danny, could have been Denny. We had one of each at some point."

"What about the mom?"

The woman wore a red turban.

"You know, it wasn't a social event," said Kit. "The moms didn't retire into the kitchen and drink coffee while the boys played. It was pure survival. Three of us would go off to run errands while the other four stood guard. That was basically it. There was very little chitchat."

She took the photo from my hand and settled back on the sofa.

"But the mom, her name was something like Meg."

"Could it have been Maggie?"

"Yes. I think that's right. Her son was a year or two older. I didn't know about the spectrum then. If I did, I would have realized he was fairly high on it. He never said much. These boys basically parallel-played way beyond the time it was age-appropriate. But I think . . ." She flicked the photo with her finger three times quickly. "Yes. He was the one with the explosive temper. He hit Quint with a toy shovel once. We had this sandbox shaped like a turtle, and all Quint did was step in it while this boy was playing there.

"The boy only came for a few months. His mother had this beautiful thick red hair. Then she was diagnosed with breast cancer, which is why she has the turban on in the picture. They didn't come much after this. I heard later she died."

"Did anyone else ever bring the boy to play group? Like his father?" I said.

"Another woman. The boy's aunt," said Kit. "But never the father."

I WAS ON to something, I thought as I left the cottage. I just didn't know what. I closed myself into my car and stuck the key into the ignition, but I didn't turn it. In the caddie yard, security lights shone down from the peak of the pro shop roof. Beyond the light lay the darkness of the golf course, the fairways a vague silver in the night.

I started the car and shifted into gear, letting the idle of the engine push it forward. Something came over me as I drew abreast of the yard, something I'd tried to keep in the background but couldn't any longer.

I turned into the yard and nosed the car to the barn door. I took my work keys from the glove compartment and got out. A sudden hiss to my right made me jump—the sprinklers on the twelfth green erupting to life. I calmed myself, taking deep breaths as the sprinklers settled into their rhythmic chuck-chuck. I unlocked the barn door and pulled it up as far as the kink in the roller track. Sometimes inaction is a virtue. If I had fixed the kink, I would have needed a flashlight, a ruler, maybe a magnifying glass. As it was, I put my leg against the track and marked the height of the kink by rubbing my hand just below the knee.

I STOPPED HOME and ran inside. The phone book had dozens of Donahues listed, but only one entry for "G & M Donahue" in Port Byram. I scribbled down the address and rushed back to the car.

The neighborhood was tight and crowded. Small houses, small yards, cars packed into driveways and lining the curbs. I found Donahue's house and, luckily enough, a spot to park diagonally across the street. A few houses glowed with the flickering blue light of TV screens, but most, including Donahue's, were dark. His was a small Cape with a shallow front yard and a driveway that ended at a stand of shrubs. A car was parked in the driveway, as far forward as possible. The time was just past midnight.

I slouched into my vigil, watching until I felt assured that the neighborhood was as quiet as it seemed. Satisfied, I pawed through the glove compartment for a penlight, then slipped out of the car and pressed the door closed behind me.

Reynaldo had described a dark sedan. As I crossed the street, the car in the shadows of the driveway resolved into a small white station wagon, a Subaru, to be exact, with a bumper sticker above the tailpipe that read, "I'd Rather Be Boating." Roger said that people often didn't see what they thought they saw, which made eyewitness testimony unreliable. I doubted there were any conditions of lighting and distance that could transform this white station wagon into a gray sedan, but I followed through anyway, measuring my knee against the bumper and playing the penlight along the rear quarter panel. The bumper was too low to have bent the door track, and the quarter panel showed no dents or scratches. I sat back on my heels, thinking. There was no way this car had been in the caddie yard the morning Rick died.

I got to my feet with the idea of heading home and nursing this blow to my theory. Far down the street, a set of headlights curved into view. I easily had enough time to cross, but something—instinct, maybe, or some subconscious perception—told me to stop. The same shrubs at the top of the driveway also formed a boundary with the neighbor's yard. I backed against them and, as the gray sedan slowed down to swing in behind the Subaru, pushed myself inside.

"Drive like that and you'll pass the road test no sweat."

George's voice sounded close. All I could see through the shrub branches were the sedan's passenger door and front tire.

The engine cut off.

"You feel better?"

The answering grunt sounded like an assent. It was a language I knew well.

"Look, you can't do what you did tonight. I can't always bail you out. What if I wasn't a cop?"

"They made fun," said Danny.

"You're right. They shouldn't. But they did. And once they did, the burden shifted to you to be a man."

I heard several rapid thuds, which I took to be the heel of Danny's hand pounding the steering wheel. George stayed silent, exercising a parental indulgence I well understood. The thuds stopped, and George opened his door. The lick of light spilling from the car almost reached my sneakers. I held my breath.

"You hungry?" said George. He closed his door, and a moment later, Danny closed his.

"Guess so."

"Me too. How 'bout I whip up some pancakes?"

"Mom's special recipe?"

"Yeah," said George. "Mom's special recipe."

I waited in the shrubs long after they went into the house and long after the light came on in the front window. Eventually, I felt safe enough to creep out. The sedan blocked me from view as I pressed my knee against the right rear bumper. The penlight showed fresh scratches at the exact right height.

I crawled through the bushes and into the neighbor's yard. Then I walked a full block in the opposite direction before crossing to the other side of the street and doubling back to my car. As I passed the house, I could see George and Danny in the window. They sat on opposite sides of a table, their heads bent almost together as they ate their midnight pancakes.

TWENTY-SEVEN

I PASSED A weird night. It reminded me of college cramming nights when, jangled by gallons of coffee, I skimmed across the surface of sleep rather than descend through the depths of its stages. Except I hadn't drunk a drop of coffee.

A thin stream of traffic whined on the interstate. The house cracked and ticked, settling as the night air mixed in. The numbers on the digital alarm clock—all threes—cast a red spell over my entire bedroom. I slid to a cool spot in the sheets. The ceiling pressed down on me, and I rolled over to bury my head under a pillow. No light, no sound. Only this:

The light is pink that morning, rising above the dark tree line beyond the fairways as Rick crosses the yard with Duke nipping along behind him. He rattles his keys, maybe drops them and sighs with exertion as he bends to pluck them off the ground. He unlocks the cart barn door and raises it smoothly on its track. Sensing a presence, he turns to see a gray sedan idling in the yard. He is confused at first; the sedan has a spotlight mounted on its mirror like an unmarked police car. But then the window slides down, and a blunt head with slick brown hair tilts outside.

Rick recognizes the boy, just as surely as someone recognizes a lover from the past, not only visually but subliminally, the incalculable organization of angles and planes and curves unmistakable over the years. Rick feels himself flush, senses a stirring in his pants. He strolls toward the open window.

"Hi," he says, or something like that.

"Get in," says the boy, or something like that, too.

Rick goes around to the passenger door and gets into the car. He sees the rosary beads hanging from the mirror, the notepad tucked into the seam of the seat. He is amused at first and then intrigued by the changes that occurred in the ten-plus years while in his own mind the boy remained a boy in the play group. The boy's arm, extended to the steering wheel, is sculpted with muscle. Peach fuzz swirls across the sharp angle of the jawline. Rick cautiously extends a hand, removes the boy's from the steering wheel, stitches the fingers together.

The boy draws Rick in, his knuckles softly caressing the side of Rick's face. But slowly the rage begins to build inside. It's been building since he first recalled what Rick did to him that day at the play group, building since he explored those devastating memories in his writing. Now the rage boils over, and he attacks, reversing Rick into a wrestling hold and squeezing his neck until the oxygen trapped in his lungs metabolizes to poison.

Outside the car, Duke whimpers. Rick slumps against the door, a thick cord of saliva on his chin. The boy drives the car into the barn. The rest is suggested by what the headlights show: golf carts, bare rafters, the coiled clothesline hanging from a hook on the wall. The boy chases Duke outside, then pulls down the barn door and works by the headlights. He rolls a cart out of line, tosses the rope over the rafters. He drags Rick from the car, his dead weight flopping, his workboots scuffing the macadam. He sits Rick directly under the rafter, bending him forward at the waist and stepping away only when the body is balanced. He quickly fashions a slipknot, fits the noose over Rick's head, and runs it tight. Then he begins to hoist Rick off the floor, pulling arm over arm, twisting the rope around his hand with each new grip. The head snaps back first, then the torso straightens, then the feet drag. The boy feels the rope biting the wood as it rasps across the edge of the rafter. Several times, he looks up to make sure the rope isn't fraying. It's not; it's a new rope, still waxy to the touch.

The boy gives one last pull, then lashes the end of the rope to a cart bumper. Rick swings free. The boy kills the headlights, plunging the barn into darkness. Morning has brightened outside, and the tiny vents beyond the rafters twinkle like distant stars. He starts the car and lifts the barn door. Duke runs in and whimpers at Rick's feet. The boy ignores him for now. He puts the car into reverse and hits something.

"Dammit," he mutters.

He pulls forward, adjusts the wheel, reverses into the yard. He jumps out of the car. There are some scratches near the back bumper, but his father will never notice, and what the hell, it's a police department car. The bigger problem is the door track, which is bent like hell. He grabs it with both hands, the same hands that strangled Rick, and twists. The track budges just enough.

He chases Duke out of the barn, forces the door shut, and drives away.

I HAD NO sensation of getting out of bed, no idea how many times I paced across the bedroom floor. I knew what I knew well enough to imagine what happened, but not well enough to make a case. I couldn't go to the Poningo PD with my theory; I didn't know what George knew, if he knew anything at all, or what he would do, if he would do anything at all, when I told him his son killed Rick. I needed to present my theory to some other authority—the DA's office, maybe, or state police investigators. For that, I needed to make sure I had every last detail straight, and there was still one more to nail down. Plus, in just a few hours, I was departing to play in a little thing called the U.S. Open.

EIGHT A.M., AND I dropped Sam off at the police station for his last counseling session with Nick before the trip. I pulled away quickly, not wanting to risk an encounter with Nick or, for that matter, George.

The next stop was the AAC. My plan, in the light of a truly glorious morning, was this: Cooperate fully with Ms.

Gauman and put in a formal request for releases. By the time I returned from the Open, I would have the identity of the poet. If my assumption turned out to be correct—and I was certain it would—I could go to the DA or the state police with every possible question already answered.

Unfortunately, the AAC was closed and didn't open till ten. So with two hours to kill, I went to the club. Good thing I did, because the girls had a going-away gift for me when they arrived at eight-thirty. We hugged and kissed while the yard went chaotic all around us.

"We're going to miss you," said Lulu.

"I'll probably be slamming my trunk on Friday," I said. It was a pro golf term, meaning that you didn't survive the thirty-six-hole cut and were heading home.

"Nonsense. You'll play great and be gone forever," said Steph. She pretended to sniffle.

"Never happen," I said, and though Steph had articulated the plan that had been in my head for years, it sounded uncomfortably final today.

I opened the box. Inside was a handkerchief with each of our four names embroidered in pink along the four sides. In the middle were "Good luck, Jen" and "Friends 4ever."

"A little high school–ish," said Cindy.

"But sweet," I said. "You guys are the greatest."

We all hugged again. My eyes filled.

Nine o'clock was closing in. Eddie-O stood in the middle of the yard, lifted his starter's pistol into the air, and squeezed off six blanks. After the reports died away, a gray sedan rolled down the hill and stopped at the edge of the patio. Sunlight glared off the windshield, hiding the driver and the possibility of dangling rosary beads from my eyes. The engine kicked down, the door opened, and Nick, not George, got out.

"Hi," he said.

"Hi," I responded.

"Plainclothes today." He lifted his arms and twirled, modeling his khakis and hunter green shirt.

I could see he was in plainclothes, but I read the statement for what it truly was: a peace offering.

"Looks good," I said.

"May I sit?" he said.

I nodded, and he dragged out a chair, seeming to calculate the exact distance to place it from mine.

"I want to apologize for last night," he said. "I was out of line."

I said nothing, just leaned forward with my elbows on the table and my hands webbed.

"I did a lot of thinking," Nick said. "Sometimes thinking can dig you too much into your own head, but I did some thinking, and here it is. We have whatever it is we have between us . . ."

I shifted involuntarily, taking a deep breath as if to speak.

"Please." He held up a hand. "Don't define it."

I settled back. He needn't have worried. The last thing I was going to do was define what we had.

"As long as we see each other in whatever social capacity we see each other," he said. "And as long as I'm counseling Sam, and as long as you're trying to help Kit Gilbert prove her husband didn't kill himself, we are going to be tripping over each other. Do you see?"

I saw. "Don't you think that's why I asked you about ethics when you first asked me to dinner?"

"We're beyond that now."

"Well beyond it, I'd say."

"And so we need to deal with the situation as it stands," he said.

"Or walk away from it."

"Would you please listen?" he said, wounded. "I want to make up for last night. Not meet you at Seaside Bobby's or come over for you to cook. A real date. You deserve it."

I did, but I didn't fancy hearing it from him right this minute.

"Sorry. I'm leaving for the Open."

"That's today already?"

I nodded.

"The other thing is that I want to help you help Kit. It's not my case, but what good is it to . . ." He searched for the right word. "To know a police officer and not ask for help?"

"I know a lot of police officers." I couldn't resist saying it and immediately took it back. "I'm kidding, Nick. Just kidding."

"What time are you leaving?"

"Noon. Assuming I can get Sam to move."

"Can we meet before?" He checked his watch. "Maybe ten minutes earlier. At the AAC."

"For what?"

"To find out who wrote that poem," he said.

Naturally, what I wanted from him last night I didn't want now.

"What about Donahue?"

"George isn't territorial about his investigations. If we find something, he'll thank us."

I doubted that. Nick scraped back his chair and stood.

"Ten to twelve," he said.

"I won't have the time."

"How about now?"

"It doesn't open till ten."

"Then we're back to ten to twelve." He came around the table and kissed me. It was a decent kiss, with only a hint of bravado. "Meet you there."

I nodded, the gesture somehow less obligatory than answering in words. Nick closed himself into his car, but before he backed up, I heard the familiar puttering of the Volvo wagon. It came into view, crossing behind Nick's car. Sometimes you can see more in a stroboscopic blink than in any intensely exhaustive study. Kit gripped the wheel as if it were a life preserver, while beside her, Quint covered his face with his hands. In that second, I saw despair.

I waited until Nick drove away before getting up from the table. If I had any chance of helping Kit, I knew one thing: I needed to find out who wrote that poem before Nick did.

TWENTY-EIGHT

COULD I HAVE gotten any luckier?

The *Maggie May* bobbed gently in its slip. There were tools scattered on the dock, but no sign of George. Danny crouched in the stern. He wore a black wet suit top and red surfer jams and buffed a new brass railing on the top of the gunwale with a cheesecloth. His bare arms, even more powerful than I imagined, worked like pistons.

I called him by name. He ignored me at first and rubbed the cheesecloth harder. By my third call, I could see his mental processes at work. He stopped rubbing. A moment later, he turned toward me but kept his eyes on the rail. A moment after that, he looked up. His eyes brushed across mine, then settled somewhere near my feet.

"I'm Jenny," I said. "I'm a friend of your dad's. May I come aboard?"

I took his silence for permission and landed lightly on

the deck. He stepped back quickly, three paces that kept the exact same distance between us.

"Is your dad around?"

"Not now," he said.

"I've visited your dad here before. You were swimming. The boat looks great. Is it finished?"

"I'm shining the rails," he said.

"They look very shiny."

I tapped the rail with the tip of my finger. Danny shot forward, rubbed the spot with the cloth, then retreated.

"Sorry. I should be more careful," I said.

He nodded. "You should."

"I actually wanted to ask you a question," I said. "I'm a part-time poetry teacher. Do you like poems?"

"Sort of," he said.

"I was at the AAC the other day. I know you go there because your dad told me."

Danny rubbed the rail harder and faster than before.

"There was a poem in the window. It was about a beach."

Danny stopped rubbing. He straightened up and let the cheesecloth drop from his hand.

"It's a fantastic poem," I said. "Do you know who wrote it?"

"I'm not supposed to . . ."

He snatched the cheesecloth and backed away. I moved after him, careful not to intrude on his personal space.

"Not supposed to what?" I said.

"Not supposed to talk." He wrapped the cheesecloth tightly around the open palm of one hand.

"About the poem?" I said.

"Anything," he said. "To anybody."

He unwound the cheesecloth and dove over the gunwale into the narrow strip of water between the *Maggie May* and the next boat. Three huge breaststrokes shot him well beyond the bow. He looked back at me with a tilt to his head that was oddly animal in its aspect, then rolled over into a crawl and swam out into the harbor.

There was a thud, and the boat shook. George was on deck, wearing cutoffs and a tank top, a plastic bag with the familiar logo of a local deli dangling heavily from one hand.

"Can you tell me what just happened?" he said.

I started to answer, but his mood was so aggressive that I didn't know what to say. Anyway, he didn't wait. He dropped the bag and strode past me to the bow. Far out in the harbor, a tiny patch of water churned. George cupped his hands to his mouth and shouted Danny's name three times, stressing the second of the two syllables in a way that gave the name its own peculiar melody. The churning stopped. Danny bobbed shoulder high. George waved, and Danny waved back. That was it. No talk. Just a reassuring signal between father and son.

George came back to the stern.

"It's Tuesday," he said. "Shouldn't you be playing in the ladies' shotgun?"

"You have a good memory." I summoned my most engaging smile.

"One of my strengths." He didn't smile back. I noticed the hint of a bruise under his right eye and flashed on the image of Danny dropping down from the basketball goal.

"I didn't play today. I'm leaving for West Virginia this afternoon. The Open. Anyway, I saw the boat was back and I wanted to say hi."

"Good luck," he said absently, and turned back toward the harbor. Danny's head bobbed, and near it was a second head, smaller and darker.

"He's skittish with new people," said George. "Closed spaces, too. A boat is not a good place to confront him."

"It wasn't a confrontation."

"Maybe not in your mind."

"I asked permission to come aboard," I said. "Maybe I misinterpreted his answer."

George raised an eyebrow. There was no "maybe" about it.

"She was up in Norwalk," he said, "having a new inboard engine installed. They turned her around pretty quick. It helps to be a cop."

"Is she finished?" I said.

"All except for a few cosmetics. I was going to take her on a shakedown cruise. But you chased my crew away."

"Look, George, I'm sorry about . . ."

He raised a hand. "It's okay."

"Can't you call Danny in?"

"It's not that simple. Now that he's in the water, he'll be stalking that seal."

Out in the harbor, the distance between the two bobbing heads had halved.

"Of course, you could be my crew," he said.

"Me?" I said. "I'd like to, George, but I don't have much time."

"It won't take long. Only out to the islands and back." He smiled.

"I suppose I can," I said, thinking this could be another chance.

"Great." He began to unwind a rope from a cleat along the gunwale. "Get those stays."

I did. Moments later, George turned the ignition, and a low rumble bubbled up from the water. I joined him at the wheel as the *Maggie May* went smoothly under way. Out in the harbor, the two heads popped to the surface. One darted away, the other shook itself into a human face. George pulled alongside Danny and cut the engine. The deck swayed, and in the sudden silence I could hear the masts creaking. Danny treaded water easily.

"This is Ms. Chase," George called. "We're going out to the islands and back. You want to stay, right?"

Danny flattened onto his back, spitting water like a cartoon whale.

"Know your limits," said George. "He's a seal, and you're not."

"It's a she," said Danny.

George shot me a quick grin, a mix of pride and amusement.

"We'll be back soon. Watch for us. Ms. Chase isn't an experienced sailor. I'll need you to guide me in and tie her up. Got it?"

Danny replied with a thumbs-up.

George gunned the engine, and we were under way again.

"Danny has a touch with animals," I said. "Befriending a seal requires patience."

"I wouldn't call it patience," said George. "They're just easier for him to deal with than people."

"Is it autism?"

George took his eyes off the water but didn't turn around all the way.

"Twenty years ago he'd have just been considered weird. Now there's a diagnosis, all kinds of support, laws in Congress."

"It's a better time to be alive," I said.

"I'm not sure all of it is good."

"Does he go to the AAC?" I said. My cell phone vibrated against my hip.

"He has been. Convenient while I'm at the job."

"I walked by the AAC the other day," I said. "There were several poems displayed in the window."

A small outboard passed us, heading in. The couple on it waved, and George waved back.

"The poems were good," I said. "One in particular. It was about a beach. Three stanzas describing different emotional views. The first two were happy, the third was dark and sad. Very sophisticated. I got the feeling that someone important to the author had died."

"I know the poem."

"Is it Danny's?"

George nodded. "It's not really about a beach. It's about his mother's death."

"I'm sorry," I said, and I was because I should have known.

We were completely beyond the golf course now. On the starboard side, the brushy heads of the marshland reeds swayed in the breeze. On the port side, a swell lifted a skiff moored below the lawn of a mansion. Ahead were the islands, shards of rocky uplifts where trees somehow had gained a foothold.

"I didn't think he had it in him," said George. "But once he started writing, it was like a dam burst." He stared at the last green buoy as we passed it. "I know what the AAC tries to do with self-expression. I'm not sure it's a good idea."

We were through the channel now. George turned to the starboard, bringing us back around the last of the islands. I had my confirmation. The poem didn't prove beyond a reasonable doubt that Danny killed Rick Gilbert. But linking it to the notes was enough to reopen an investigation, maybe enough to get Kit her money.

George steered a course between the islands and the marshlands. The *Maggie May* moved so slowly, I could feel each stroke of the pistons. There was nothing pretty about the islands, just rocks, scraggly trees, gobs of seaweed thrown up by high tides and dried white by the sun. On the largest of them were the rotted remains of an old shack.

I squeezed the cell phone from my pocket. The readout showed a missed call from Sam. I opened and closed the lid quickly, bringing back the clock. Up ahead, buoys marked the channel.

The engine began to labor. George revved it higher, and the entire boat trembled. He eased off and revved again, but the engine coughed and died. The silence was profound.

"Dammit!" said George. He twisted the ignition, but the engine wouldn't turn over.

"Dammit!" he said again, and slapped the wheel.

"What's wrong?" I said.

He came back and leaned deeply over the stern rail.

"Can you swim?" he said.

"Not well," I said.

"Seaweed's choked the screw," he said. "We'll need to go down there and untangle it."

"Both of us?"

"Don't know. Maybe. I'll need to see first."

George pushed himself off the rail, dropped an anchor over the stern, and pulled the rope taut. Up at the bow, he dropped another anchor and pulled that rope taut, too. Then he came back and set an open toolbox against the gunwale.

"Hopefully, I can do this without both of us in the water," he said.

I hoped so, too. Swimming for me was a weak breast-stroke across the low end of the club pool. Two laps and I was winded. I hated natural bodies of water, seaweed, anything out of my depth. This was all three.

"You hand me whatever I ask for."

"Will do," I said.

George flipped himself over the stern rail, slicing into the water feet first. I shuddered as he dissolved into the darkness. The water here was deeper than I thought, and long moments passed before he bobbed back to the surface. He took several hyperventilating breaths, then dove. I couldn't see him, so I counted. Then I stopped counting. Finally, he burst to the surface, air exploding from his mouth.

He caught his breath, hyperventilated, and dove again. I didn't count this time. He knew what he was doing and didn't need me advising him, or cautioning him, or even worrying about him. I looked out toward the channel. Boats passed in both directions, and I wondered if we looked obviously in trouble. One boat making for the Sound seemed to pause as a splash rose behind it. Then George broke the surface.

"I think I have it," he said between breaths. "There's a knife in the toolbox. It's curved like a carpet cutter."

I pawed through the tools and handed the knife over the rail. George kicked himself up to grab it.

"Thanks," he said, and dove again.

The boat trembled. I imagined George far below, hacking the long, sinuous strands and then unraveling them from the screw. The trembling stopped, and a moment later he surfaced. He spat a mouthful of water and hungrily sucked at the air.

"Are you all right?" I said.

He mumbled something unintelligible, and I shuddered again. Hyperventilating itself was dangerous. Add the exertion of hacking at seaweed and he could pass out.

"Bungee cord," he gasped. "Give me one."

I didn't ask why he needed a bungee. I just grabbed one and reached it over the rail. He waved at it, unable to kick himself high enough to reach it. This better be all, I thought. He's getting tired. I leaned out as far as I could and dangled the bungee. His fingers brushed the metal hook.

"Take your time," I said.

He sank as if to gather himself, drew some water into his mouth, and spat it out. Then, in an instant, he shot up from the water, grabbed my wrist, and pulled me headfirst over the side. Water shot up my nose and plugged my ears.

I flailed my arms, not knowing up from down. Finally, George wrestled me to the surface. I gagged water, gasped for air. The sudden plunge had caught me between breaths.

"George—" I coughed. "That wasn't funny."

And then I knew, from the look on his face, that it wasn't meant to be.

"George?" I said.

"Why did you come here?"

"To say hi."

He spun me around, bent my arms behind my back. Pain erupted in my shoulder. I screamed, but he dunked me. Water filled my mouth. He pulled me up. I coughed, the salty taste stinging my throat.

"Don't insult me. You came to see Danny. You wanted to get him by himself."

"No. I told you. I saw the boat. I wanted to say hi."

He yanked my head back by the hair.

"What were you saying to him when he jumped into the water?"

"Nothing."

He yanked again.

"Okay, okay. Stop. I asked him about the poem."

"What's so damn important about that poem?"

"I used to teach English. I was impressed."

"That's bullshit. You didn't know Danny went to the AAC. You didn't even know he was autistic until I just told you."

"Kit told me," I said.

"You're asking Kit Gilbert about my son?" He let go of my hair. I drifted away, but he grabbed my arm.

"She showed me pictures of a play group," I said. "Long time ago. I recognized Danny."

"Why were you talking to Kit about a play group?"

"It came up."

"It came up how? With Rick?"

"I think Rick. Some of the boys—"

He pulled me hard against him, and suddenly everything I thought I knew seemed totally irrelevant and completely absurd.

"You want to know about the play group?" His voice hissed in my ear. "Maggie saw a sign posted at the A and P. She thought it sounded like a good idea, so she joined. I never knew the where or the who or the when. Even the meetings at our house, I was always at the job. When Maggie got sick, my sister took Danny. It was one of those times that Danny came back different. I didn't make any connection. Me, a cop, and I didn't clue in on my own kid. It wasn't until Danny started writing on that laptop they gave him that I found out what that bastard did to him."

Something circled my wrists. The bungee.

"You're just like that goddamn pervert, coming out to take advantage of Danny."

"I didn't touch him."

"There are other ways of taking advantage."

"I wouldn't—"

"You should have left my son alone."

"George, I didn't do anything to him. We can ask him."

"Too late. Nobody abuses my son anymore. Ask Rick."

"George. Please. Don't. Nick knows—"

"Nick doesn't know a damn thing. He's been humoring you to get in your pants."

"But I told Charlie. Roger, too."

"I'll take my chances." He dunked my head three times violently. When he stopped, I was choking, crying. How stupid of me to think I could solve anyone's problems.

"I won't . . ." I couldn't finish the thought.

He pushed me away. I drifted, trying to scream and trying to keep my head above water. I couldn't do both, and then I couldn't do either.

The water closed over me. I kicked, broke the surface again. *George!* I screamed. But it was my mind, not my mouth, that screamed. I slipped under as he flipped himself onto the boat. I kicked again, just enough for a quick sip of air and a glimpse of him watching me, his arms dangling over the rail.

Gravity sucked me down. The sky scrambled as the water thickened above me. I knew what he was going to do. He was going to watch my accidental drowning from the boat, and when it was over he would remove the bungee.

I managed to kick myself to the air one more time. *You'll never get away with it,* I said in my mind. But even this disembodied voice, the voice I'd heard in my head all my life, was weakening. I twisted my wrists. He could take away the bungee, but if there were abrasions on my wrists, maybe someone would notice. And ask questions. Funny how small one's world can shrink.

The water darkened around me. The sun dimmed to a pale, January yellow. My chest began to burn. I thought of the day Sam was born and how I held him for a brief moment in the recovery room and watched the drumskin of flesh beating on his skull and pledged my life to him. I remembered the day we took him home from the hospital and how a sudden thunderstorm trapped the three of us in our car outside our apartment. We sat until the rain shut off because we didn't want him to get wet.

Baby Sam faded. The seaweed rose to envelop me, its sandpaper feel oddly pleasant. My lungs burned. If only I could take a breath, one breath, maybe this wouldn't be so bad.

I opened my mouth. A single large bubble wormed out, and water poured in. It wasn't salty or cold, but sweet and warm.

Far away, a cloud blotted the dimming sun.

You win, Roger. Take care of Sam, was my dying thought.

Then suddenly I wasn't sinking anymore but rising. Rising toward a white light. And in that white light, something swam for me. A seal.

There are seals in heaven, I thought. And closed my eyes.

TWENTY-NINE

MY ARMS PUMPED. My chest pounded. A white light blinded me.

My head tilted back. Hot air poured into my mouth. My stomach caught.

I rolled sideways and hacked up a mess of dirty water. I was breathing real air. My stomach caught again, and I chucked more dirty water onto a wooden deck that suddenly formed beneath me.

I sat up.

George stood at a wheel attached to a control panel with a tiny windshield. He was barefoot, dripping wet. A huge canvas sail flapped above me. I was on a boat. I remembered now: George tried to kill me. I looked side to side, orienting myself between the islands and the marshland. Last thing I knew, I was drowning. How did I get here?

Something rustled behind me. Against the sun, the

squat, powerful form was neither man nor boy, human nor beast. He stepped out of the glare.

"Danny?" I said.

"You're heavy when you're wet." A strand of seaweed hooked over one ear.

"But you were back at the harbor."

"I hitched a ride," he said. "Swam from the channel. Helped Daddy save you."

He leaned down, slipped his arm beneath my knees and shoulders, and lifted me easily onto the cushions along the port gunwale.

"You helped your daddy save me?" I said.

"You rest," he said. "We're going home now."

Danny went to the helm. George stepped aside and let him take the wheel. I couldn't read George's expression. He certainly didn't resemble the madman who had throttled me in the water and left me to drown, but he wasn't quite chastened, either.

Danny started the engine. The vibration traveled up my spine and spread to my shoulders and down my arms. It felt good, like when Charlie rubbed me with his thumbs. George hauled in the bow anchor and ignored me when he came back to pull in the stern. He rejoined Danny and, with one hand on the boy's shoulder, pointed out buoys and landmarks as we turned into the channel.

I sat up and hugged my knees, chilled by a sudden realization. Yes, Danny had saved me, and yes, I was going home. But the protection of Danny's presence wouldn't stay with me forever, because the simple fact was I knew too much. I needed to think of some way to inoculate myself, maybe broadcast my suspicions so that nothing, not even an accident, could occur without setting off alarms. Roger, I decided. I needed to talk to Roger. Despite what he could gain from my untimely demise, he was the only person I knew cynical enough to believe my story. I squeezed the cell phone from my pocket. It was dead.

George took over the wheel as we entered the harbor. He pulled past the dock, goosed the engine to stop, and then slowly reversed into the slip. Danny scrambled around the gunwale, tossing white rubber bumpers over the side. Neither of them noticed Nick standing on the dock.

Nick jumped aboard before the boat was completely in the slip. I tried to stand, thinking maybe he could get me off the boat before George stopped me. But the swaying deck and my own unsteady balance put me in a swoon. I grabbed a hunk of shirt as I collapsed back onto the cushion and pulled Nick with me.

"George tried to kill me," I whispered into his ear. "He tried to make it look like a drowning. Danny saved me."

Nick pried open my fingers and brushed the wrinkles out of his shirt.

"He killed Rick, too," I said. "He told me as much."

Nick said nothing. He went up to the helm just as George cut the engine. The silence not only ended the pleasant vibration, but left me feeling naked, completely at the mercy of others. The two men shook hands and clapped shoulders, then exchanged pleasantries about the boat, Nick saying it looked good and George saying there were still kinks to work out.

They strolled up to the bow, where they spoke for a

long time and more than occasionally glanced my way. I didn't like this. I didn't know what George could be telling Nick and what Nick, as his subordinate, would believe or not believe. Worse, the image of two men discussing my fate in private frightened the hell out of me. I'd already been the victim of male machinations twice in my life.

"Feel better?"

Danny knelt on the dock behind me, wrapping a stay around a cleat.

"Yes, Danny," I said. "Thank you."

The discussion at the bow ended. Nick and George came back to the stern. Nick opened his radio.

"This is mobile ten at the town docks," he said. "I'm going to need a squad car with one female officer. Also an ambulance. I have a report of a near accidental drowning here."

"What? Nick!" I couldn't contain myself. "That was no accident. He tried to kill me."

George smiled, shook his head. His obvious ploy was to paint me as crazy.

"He pulled me in," I said. "Bungeed my hands so I couldn't swim."

"Like I told you," George said to Nick, "Danny and I were getting ready for a shakedown cruise. Jenny came by, and we invited her to come along. We had some trouble out there. I'll admit that. And I should have insisted she wear a life vest. She was trying to help when she must have fallen overboard. I didn't even know it happened. If it hadn't been for Danny."

I couldn't believe my ears. Well, actually, I could.

George would have said anything to talk his way out. What I couldn't believe was that Nick was swallowing this crap. I turned to the only person who could verify at least some of the truth. Danny still knelt on the dock, wrapping and unwrapping a rope around a cleat. He didn't say a word, didn't even lift his head, because he'd never contradict his father.

The squad car and ambulance pulled in beside the harbormaster's shack. Two cops and three EMTs with a gurney ran down the gangway. Now I knew why Nick had specified a female officer. He not only didn't believe my story, he also was going to arrest me. Why not? I hadn't done anything except turn this tiny corner of the world on its head.

Well, I wasn't going to submit willingly. I tried to stand, but another swoon hit me and I fell back onto the cushions.

Nick climbed onto the dock. He spoke first to the EMTs, then to the cops. I tried to listen, but my head was aswirl. My stomach heaved, and I leaned over the side for a retch that never came. Three sets of feet hit the deck. I turned back from the side. Nick loomed over me, with the two cops directly behind him.

"You okay?" he said.

I thrust out my arms, my wrists together.

"Do it and be done with it," I said.

He winked, then straightened up and turned to George.

"George," he said, "you're under arrest."

A smile bloomed slowly on George's face. "You're crazy," he said.

Nick unfastened the handcuffs from his belt. "Turn around, George. We'll see how crazy I am."

"I told you what happened. She fell overboard."

"You told me a lot of things."

"You believe her over me? I thought you were just after her ass."

"Turn around, George, and shut up."

George turned. Nick grabbed his wrists together, cuffed them, and then signaled for the two cops to take him away. Danny scrambled up from the dock and fell into step behind his father. The female officer let go of George and put her arm on Danny's shoulder. I expected Danny to do something. He'd reacted to the insults at the skate park, and seeing his father led away in handcuffs was some kind of insult. But he followed meekly up the gangway to the squad car. He must have known.

Nick settled onto the cushion and put his arm around me. I melted against him, relieved.

"You know, Jenny, I really did listen to you when you talked about Rick Gilbert. I figured someone like you wouldn't get involved in something like that without good reason. When I found out Danny Donahue wrote that poem, I knew you were on to something."

"Could have fooled me. When you called for a female officer, I thought you were going to arrest me," I said.

"I wanted George to think that, too. I needed backup, and the female officer actually was for Danny. I had no idea what either of them would do."

"What did George tell you?"

Nick unwound himself from my body and stood.

"Let's just say the more he talked, the deeper he dug himself," he said. "But right now, you need medical attention."

The EMT crew came aboard and lashed me to the gurney.

"I thought you believed his story," I said. "About my accident."

"Jenny, look at your wrists."

I held them up. They were chafed red from the bungee.

"I rubbed them together," I said. "If I was going to die, I needed to leave some evidence behind."

"Smart lady," said Nick.

I closed my eyes and felt the gurney bearing me away. I could fall in love with a guy who called me smart.

THIRTY

I PHONED SAM from the ER.

"I called you like about five hours ago," he said. "Talk about me and my cell phone."

"Sorry, Sam. That won't happen again. Promise. Why did you call?"

He had called because he was looking for a particular T-shirt he wanted to bring on the trip.

"We're not going to the Open, Sam."

"We're not?"

"I had an accident. I'm in the hospital, and I need to stay overnight for observation."

"What happened?"

"I took a nosedive into water that was over my head."

"But, Mom, you can't swim."

"Tell me about it," I said.

. . .

NICK CAME TO my room that night at the tail end of visiting hours. I had an IV in my arm and an oxygen line clipped to my nose, but I scooted over enough so he could sit on the edge of the bed. We chatted first about my health, and after I assured him I was fine, he began to rub the inside of my thigh through the sheets. I stopped him immediately, not because it didn't feel good, but because I didn't want to start anything we couldn't finish.

"What the hell were you thinking," he said, "getting on that boat with George?"

"I didn't get on the boat with George. When I got there it was only Danny. I asked him about the poem, he jumped into the water, then George appeared. I thought Danny was the killer, not George."

"I questioned George for two hours," said Nick. "He sent those notes to Rick and Reynaldo, Rick for obvious reasons, Reynaldo because he could place George's car at the scene. He used Danny's AAC laptop to do it. Sydnie was Danny's default font. George probably didn't know enough to change it. Danny's account of the abuse was on the laptop. One of our techs at the job said that file was opened at least fifty times. George must have obsessed about it. We figure he watched Rick for two weeks before he made his move."

He patted my knee and quickly withdrew his hand. "I also found Reynaldo's statement buried in George's desk. He said everything you said he said."

"So much for the lying illegal immigrant theory," I said.

"Touché," said Nick.

. . .

THE HOSPITAL RELEASED me late the next morning. Charlie drove me home and installed me in my own bed, where I was under doctor's orders to remain for the next two days. At noon, the national golf cable channel began its Open telecast. My playing group already had finished with a 75 and a 78. Would I have done any better? I'd never know.

"Almost forgot." Charlie reached into his pants pocket. "This e-mail came for you at the shop. One of the caddies showed me how to print it."

It read: "I'm at the Open; where are you?"

I bit my lower lip to stop the corners of my mouth from turning down.

"Adoring fans?" said Charlie.

"I'd like to think so," I said.

THE HEARING WAS the last week before Labor Day. I waited outside the courtroom for an hour before I was called to testify. Kit sat at one counsel's table with Terry Silverman, and Danny Donahue sat at the other with a female attorney who had been appointed as his law guardian. George was in the first row of the gallery, flanked by two guards from the county jail. I cut him a hard stare, but he didn't meet my eye. In fact, he shriveled under my gaze.

Terry Silverman questioned me first.

"Ms. Chase, how long have you known Kit Gilbert?"

"Several years."

"And during that time, have you had an opportunity to observe her parenting skills?"

"I have."

"And how would you characterize them?"

"Superior," I said.

Terry Silverman sat down. The judge, a grandfatherly gentleman totally devoid of pomposity, called for the law guardian.

"No questions," she said.

I stepped down from the stand and took a seat in the last row of the gallery. Since there were no more witnesses, the judge read his ruling from the bench.

"Based on the testimony, and considering the best interests of the child, the petition is granted," he said. "I hereby award temporary custody of Daniel Donahue to Kit Gilbert."

CHARLIE AND I were on the practice tee, imparting our considerable golf knowledge to a clinic of beginners, when the huge semitrailer moving van raked through the willow branches along the driveway. Kit's comparatively tiny Volvo station wagon followed close behind.

We had discussed the upshot often over the last few days, Danny Donahue living with his abuser's family and the arrangement funded by the money his abuser left behind.

"My idea," I now confessed. "Roger helped with the arrangements."

"Ironic," said Charlie.

"I prefer poetic justice," I said.

Charlie groaned.

"That's not a pun," I said. "It's a bon mot."

"I know it's a bon mot," he said. "I was a French major."

"I thought you were pre-med."

The moving van turned onto the Post Road and slowly gathered speed as it crossed beyond the practice range. Kit gunned the Volvo and overtook the lead. In a moment, they were gone.

One of the beginners smacked a ball sideways, narrowly missing someone farther down the line. Her stance was all wrong, but before I could break away to correct it, Charlie crooked his elbow around my neck.

"You done good, kid," he said into my ear.

"You know, Charlie, I think I did."